The Wind Beneath the Willow

The Wind Beneath the Willow
Emma Roshioru

ISBN: 979-8-218-19150-4

References to historical events, real people, or real places are used
fictitiously. Names, characters, and places are products of the author's
imagination.

Cover image aspects:
Michele Roshioru
Drew Hays / Unsplash
© Getty Images

First printing edition 2023.

To my family, whose endless encouragement has allowed me to endure

The Wind Beneath the Willow

1

It was the summer month—the warm breeze, the orange sun, and the green grass, when I laid my eyes upon what was the utmost perfect and complete, unaware beauty. In the depths of my wicked heart, she was the light and the joy that rang in the back of my soundless mind. Only a madman, only one of pure insanity yet genius, could see she was the most beautiful girl to walk the grass and dirt of this earth's ground and breathe the air of the wind just shaking the willow tree.

It was in that summer month that I filled the sorrowful hole in my soul; the season I became complete. Something about the summer air, the smell of it, the feel of it. It was the wind blown onto my face while riding down Main in the car, the kids riding their bicycles down a hot paved street, the dogs barking, the children laughing while their fathers sit and read, the fact that in all the noise, there was still a soundless town. The freeness of the season, the beauty of its seemingly never-ending joy.

Summer is of my favorite seasons; it was hers too.

2

I thought the countryside would be the bane of me, but the hills where we ran and the river in which we played proved me immensely wrong. You see, it was in the countryside where I found Charlotte, and with Charlotte lies the worst of my sins yet the entirety of my heart.

It all began when I left the city and presumed a law post in the South. I was to be a small-town lawyer. The city had become too gruesome to bear, and I needed a new start which I believed I could find in a small town in the lower half of the country. It took approximately six weeks and two days to organize my position, previous upholdings, and new circumstances. I left Maine on the fifteenth of April in the year 1942 and found myself in Georgia only seven days later. I bought a house with a plot of land, and the worst of shape a house could possibly be in. I did this so that over the summer, when I had yet to make acquaintances or presume my job, I'd still maintain a very full and busy life. The house was to be two levels with white paint, green shutters, a tin roof, and of course, equipped with the southern classic, a wrap-around porch for me, myself alone to sit and read. Although, it was in that summer month that I felt an unexplainable happiness, a feeling of solitude. You see, it was the Buddha himself who first realized nirvana, the state of profound peace, free from the fires of suffrage. I explain this concept only as I am completely positive that it was in this month that I myself reached nirvana.

Today I write to you as the summer months seemed to have all but faded away, but what awaits you—the story of my little sin—my soul in ink before you.

3

Alas, I arrive this fateful morning, quite almost the afternoon now that I think about it, to the main road of the town of which I shall take up my life from here forth. With not a moment to take in my surrounding sights, I set straight for the main mart to ask for directions. The man to greet me at the counter within the store—a short, most awkward man dressed in a simple collared shirt and glasses which hold the reflection of his front sign, almost immediately calls for a young man to drive me to my new home. The man stocking shelves nearly tumbles over, all while attempting to greet me. We let ourselves outside and to the store car, beginning our departure swiftly with no time for discussion. Now, moments have passed and upon driving aimlessly with my driver asking such questions as to where I am from, and when told the answer asking, "Why would you be here?" I only simply and blandly reply out of sincerity. Only now, in surpassing minutes of such superfluous discussion, he has since decided to ask me the address of where he should be headed. From the first remarks of this town and of the people situated within it, I feel no affirmation in my recently cemented decision.

Having driven through most of the town, which seems to have the capacity of one block, consisting of no more than three stores, one for clothing, one for food, and the last for any other miscellaneous necessity. A restaurant, a gas station, a school, a fire station, and a medical care center amass the surplus square footage, the rest simply homes for the residents of such a "town." Maine was not exceptionally intriguing on its own either, though in re-pondering such a previous conceptualization, it seems to be Rome in comparison. We did happen to drive past the courthouse, the only inhabitant of the town to be any bit eye-catching. I am to begin my work as the town's attorney in precisely three months, and as that thought occurs to me, so does the very fact that I shall be alone for those three months, which seems to be becoming of concern. It appears to me that at such a rate, the only activity I will be taking any part in is the work to be done on my home. This was expected, but so it seems, as the rest of my life has worked out, that the slight underlying hope which may have taken form shall perhaps be silenced in a very singular thought.

I believe the young man driving has been carrying on some conversation with himself all about the town not looking all so appealing, but truly being a gem. Although, all I can hear is a muffled version of his voice in the background of what white noise fills my mind. The town's bleakness has almost matched my own; the empty fields, the houses so far from the roads, and the next home has set a mood of isolation, a dry seclusion. Finally, I am broken from the white noise as the man turns to say, "This is it." And so, he sits there as I work to grab my luggage (what I have of it), and upon beginning to walk away, he only continues to sit there waiting. How foolish I must be to be so unobservant of his desire for money, payment for his monologue on four wheels. I oblige, of course, tossing the coinage his way. Finally, he drives off, and once again, I am alone.

4

As I can finally break my stare from the ground, I look up to my mailbox, broken in its own, allotting an image of the house's shape in my mind. I turn to the gruesome walk the driveway is to prevail. A long grey road, lined by willows on each side, so long I can barely see the house at the end. I begin the walk, only accompanied by the white noise once again and the few birds above. Though the town, its inhabitants, the endless space, and my slight hopes seem to be as grey as the ground I walk upon, I feel a certain serenity I have not felt on any day of my life before.

As I continue my walk down that long road, I can all the sudden see a glimpse of what I am to call my home. And in only a few paces more, I have arrived at the foot of the house, large in width and in height, wood once painted white, shutters held by a single nail, windows on the brink of shatter, a porch consisting of missing planks; but a yard that stretches on all sides, luscious green grass that appears as though only the most esteemed were meant to walk upon it. The home's camouflaged beauty, undiscovered by the standard eye, and as I stand looking at the house, I can't help but see a reflection of myself, tired and worn, yet fringed with capability. In the southern air, blowing the branches of the willows which line my drive, my sorrowful self may feel complete. With not a moment more, I depart from the foot of the home to discover its further inner beauty (most literally). Holding the knob inside my hand, I am frozen, unable to brace the very house which I am allowing to possess my life from this moment on, so I stand, contemplating this day and moment, as I finally find the strength to turn the knob and step foot into my new world. At first sight, just as its outer appearance, the inside is large with ceilings that soar above my head, a large staircase to my right, and a drawing room to my left, which I walk through opening a door in the room's corner which leads me to the kitchen. In the kitchen, there are many cabinets, countertops, a large sink, and a very large table. A table so large, it should act as a constant reminder of my loneliness in this house, but as I look up from my hand lying on the table, I look through two large glass doors into the luscious yard and I must pause for a moment to be accompanied by the serene feel once again. It has become a fact, at this moment, that when I look out to nothing other than God's pure and natural creation, I should feel full and not so lonely. And so, though that table now behind me shall ridicule my lonesome self for every time I may sit at its side, I shall catch a glimpse of the grass, the green, luscious grass, and feel not as lonely. Caught up in my thoughts, I suppose as I have somehow managed to float through what was left of the first floor, and now it seems I have found myself in the foyer once again. Positioning my eyes to gaze upon the large staircase, I succumb to my extreme weariness. It is for this reason, I grab my few bags and walk each step of that staircase to the second floor in hopes of finding a bed. Turning to my right lies a hall that, when entered, looks straight to a window facing the branches of a tree. To the right, a bathroom, and to the left is what is to be my bedroom. The room is filled with three windows; two on the back wall and one to my right, beneath this window on my right I find a dresser. I place my largest suitcase on top of this dresser and catch the top just as it falls open towards the window. Projecting my eyes upward to catch a glimpse of a tree branch, and beyond that, a home. I fix my eyes to find the only home situated near my own. My only neighbor. What a pity. I am so close to having a yard stretching only to tranquility on all sides, but alas, urbanization must fault my decree. The time seems to have become 5:33 pm. Seeing as it has become a struggle to hold my eyes open, I decide it best to unload my toothbrush, comb, soap, and pajamas, along with my bedding to prepare myself and my bed for a night of sleep, in preparation for the crude reality of what work is needed to be done to this house beginning in the morning.

5

I slept that night without a single dream or thought but awoke to a volcano of notions erupting as soon as the light from the windows hit my eyelids. I silenced my mind and my worries for just long enough to sit myself up in that hard bed, pick up my pocket watch from the window seal and rub my eyes as if to enhance my vision to further awaken myself to the realization that the time is now 6:32 am. With a vigorous breath, I know now I most certainly need curtains. I make my way trudging through the hall, down the stairs, to be awakened once more to yet another realization, I have no food in any room of this house. I barely have any belongings at all. I have only brought three suitcases, one large, two of a more medium size, but the rest of my livelihood is on its way and is to be arriving two to three weeks from today. These factors and the idea I had for a peaceful country morning accompanied by no other than myself led me to drag my weary self up those beautifully steep and tiring stairs to change and prepare myself for my departure. Making it to the bathroom, dousing my face with the coldest of water, letting out a slight wince, leading to my immediate flee for a towel. Now much livelier, I search for my most impressionable uniform, my cream button up and dark brown trousers. The clothing uncovered at last. I sit on the bed in the same position as before, pulling my shoes out from under the edge of the bed, adjusting my right shoe onto my foot, again repeating the process with my left; I complete the simple task feeling so accomplished, seeing as my tiredness has had me infeasible to any form of activity. I sit only for a few moments more, looking out my window upon the rising sun, its rays shining so bright through the trees, reflecting off the dew on the grass, causing the ground to look as if it were a million diamonds, so rich, so luxurious while still maintaining its natural essence. The time has now just become 6:46 am, and my stomach has seemed to catch a glimpse of the time as well as I can gather from its disturbing rumble. Soon enough, I make my way out of my bedroom door, to the right, down the stairs, and to the front door leaving home now at the time of 6:52 am. The country at 6:52 am is bare; with not a single soul in sight, the birds nearly awake themselves, and the sun just starting to climb over the trees. For the first time since my childhood, I find myself walking in the direct middle of the road without a worry for cars or anything for that matter. The feeling of this action though thought to be exhilarating is most peaceful—the coolness of the air, the slight dew, the sky, colors of yellow and mixtures of blue. I make this walk in the center of the road to reach the corner store, the store with the most awkward man in search of food (most importantly) but also sandpaper, cleanser, rags, paint, a few nails, and screws, an assortment of equipment to aid me in the beginning of the work to the house. I stand in this store only accompanied by none other than the awkward man dressed in his same untucked uniform, standing about in the exact same manner as if he had not moved but an inch since our last meeting. He asks me, "Are you sure your collection there is just for one man, or do you plan on making some stops on your way home?" I look up from my reading of the labels to insert, "And are you sure you are running a business or a trial?" The man, subject to my harsh blunder which pillages the morning of its affirmation, acquires a face nearly as red as that of the rising sun's rays and an attitude just as nearly that of a nun's. I check out my most 'non-cohesive' arrangement and leave that most awkward man to his store. The time, just becoming 7:32 am, and still not but a soul in sight. I presume, though stereotypical, I believed inhabitants of the country would be awake for country tasks. Though it appears as I make my walk home, I have made yet another realization, this town has neither chickens nor pigs in the backyards running about, and for another moment in my life, this morning being the first time, I have achieved the role of the most productive man in the entirety of the town. Astonishing! It has only been in just an hour that I have been able to accomplish two things I have never been able to do since my childhood or in my life in its capacity. In my singularity, I have so much accomplishment for which I now know that Zoroaster, the Buddha, countless other religious monumentaries, and other self-isolated achievers are right in their realizations. In the midst of such a philosophical awakening, I realize, for my journey back to my home, that I had not but a feeling of the grueling pace or of the weight of my luggage, the walk not so exhausting or forsaken. It must be some poison in the country's morning air that allows me to be so buoyant. Reaching home, I place my bags down upon the leaf-covered porch to unlock my door. Picking up the bags only for them to open, spreading about upon my feet. My buoyancy broken with the tears at the brown sack's bottom. My volatile self unleashed, "Damn bags!" With the door now open, I pick up my items few by few, making my trip three times that of what was anticipated, placing each item upon the top of the kitchen table. Making my way through the foyer one last time, I slam the front door, hearing a single shingle fall from the side of the home in doing so. Walking through my office in mere avoidance of that mimicking foyer, I trace back to yet another disaster upon re-entering my kitchen. With haste, I begin dusting the cabinetry, which fills the entire left and back sides of my kitchen's walls, in preparation for the filling of the cabinets with my purchases.

Come to find out, such a task takes a near forty minutes to complete in order to achieve an adequate cleaning. But alas, I begin stocking the cabinet shelves with my most disheveled items. Above the sink, which is found on the wall to the left of the wall accompanied by the glass doors, centered between dark wooden cabinetry, lies a window. To the left of this window is where I begin my stocking, piling my bread, coffee beans, and crackers into the shelves found within. Turning my back to set my eyes upon my most stupid action—cheese, jam, and vegetables galore. An act so delirious, as in my cleaning and stocking, had I ceased to come upon a refrigerator. Scanning the kitchen again- stove, yes. Sink, of course. Cabinets, a plenty. Another relatively long table, check. No refrigerator. Shockingly true, yet not any more than that of my level of ignorance, or shall I say, entitlement on my part. I come to face no other choice than to leave the items on the table to collect dust until I can stumble upon a garbage pail. In such a search, I have only brought myself to further my cleaning efforts, having each table dusted and doused with a wood cleaner of a generic odor which was the only one to be found in the store. Though, now, still I remain in the kitchen, scrubbing that long table against the wall. What is its use being for so long? Preparing food, holding a sack of flour while one may dance across the kitchen floor to their mixing bowl on the other side? A bar, which when seated, forces one to stare into nothing but brick with dust clinging on for its life? Down the rabbit hole, I fall into a precession of ludicrous questions which only take the place of what would be the white noise. I find it best to carry my speculations with me as I fall, for in losing myself in my own mind, I find myself awake to the next room already halfway cleaned. A grand room one may have used at a time for dining. A room so large, of papered walls, equipped with a less spectacular chandelier-like structure. Nothing left in its space other than the ghosts that may have once danced beneath the once gleaming lights. Nothing now but a large rectangular structure hidden behind a decaying sheet. Uncovering the disguised piece, I find a mirror as large as a door frame with gold all around its sides, quite the Parisian design. Perhaps the former owner was the Marie Antoinette of the town. Perhaps a French ambassador who made their home in this house and plenty more across the world.

Cleaning to me is a monotonous task which only provides the time for an escape, the rabbit hole to which at any moment I offer myself and my thoughts. Though at this moment, the idea which has arisen is the question of how useless this room should be to me. The room, quite humorous, like its counterpart, the kitchen table. A man, alone with no friends, not even a familiarity, my family not to be found in Georgia or in the United States as of that. My father and mother happen to live in Nottingham, I suppose I did as well once. I moved away from them for what seems to be so long ago, in my teenage years to live with my aunt in the state of Maine as a result of nothing more than my parents' most globetrotting attitude toward life. Upon living in Maine, my aunt became my nearest companion, with only one friend who I found myself compatible with. My aunt filled the shape of the empty shoes which my mother and father left behind each time they packed their bags and ran off to some other far-away place. This latest year, my aunt fell very ill, an illness which came abruptly and took her nearly as fast. As my aunt was forced to leave this earth, my friend (singular) his name, Martin, moved to care for his father who fell into a similar illness, though his father lived in Montana. Why such a choice of state, I would not know. And so, in just nearly eight months, it appears I have been left with the pain of my aunt's death and the loss of a friend who remains on earth. What may be worse—a loss both permanent and complete, or one that still may waver and is only lost in a choice of forgetting what life came before such change? The difference being, one no longer has an address, and the other has one anew. What is there to live for, you may ask of me, the law? This question had become all the more evident to myself on the day in which I stopped looking for cars before crossing the road, forcing myself to the realization that all was gone for me in Maine. Except it was in Maine and in Nottingham that I found all I had ever known. This is why I made the decision to abandon all I had known and move to the first place that would take me. That is a small town laid away in the marshes of Georgia where I was offered a position as a lawyer. In Maine, we lived in quite a small home, humble as she used to call it. She kept up with the cleaning, even the handyman duties, as she felt it kept her young. Therefore today, I teach myself as I am lost for means of familiarity. Exciting, if I should think about it. Hopeless, if I should think slightly differently.

The next room, a continuation of the grandeur. Practically resembling the first but decorated in shades of midnight blue and gold. Quite the façade. I am sure this homeowner must have been an aristocrat of sorts or one of extreme and dreamy ridiculousness. This room is filled with many more items, all covered in sheets near deterioration, some of which I uncovered to find lavish pieces of dark wood and red velvet. Despite the shape of each of the pieces, I find myself grateful for the sight of furnishings considering the amount I have left behind. I only had my desk, bed frame, and mattress brought before I arrived. The rest is to arrive soon. Despite my groaning over the dust and the slightly rotted condition, truly, the interior is not in such horrible shape, half of what I expected based on the home's exterior. I have planned to spend just as long as I need on the interior repairs; cleaning and painting, for when upon final arrival of all of my belongings I may fill my home with items that may make it a little less empty. Maybe a bit dismaying with the loss of so much open space, though dusty (as I have expressed), a home open, without the least bit of clutter, something my aunt always wished a house to be.

6

Believing I had started my day so early, I had blown through it without a single pause. The time has since become 7:58 pm, but being in the South in the summer, the sun has just begun to set. This is the moment of realization that all I have eaten in the day is dust. Currently cleaning the staircase, I make my descent from that sixth step to which I was cleaning and head to that embarrassingly stocked shelf to the left of my sink. I make myself crackers and tuna with only an ounce of pride on the side—a dinner fit for a king—if that king happened to be of a rat pack. Nevertheless, filling and a sustainable end to my day.

Getting up from the kitchen table, I step forward to the glass doors and watch the sun descend from its high seat in the clouds. And I wonder, does it ever get lonely for the sun and the moon? Day after day watching the world live, to be in love, to have happiness as they stay alone, only crossing each other's paths once a day. Maybe it is that the sun does not only watch a happy family walk their dog through the park, laughing, swinging their child along, but the sun also watches a wife abused by her husband while the child hides behind the couch and is it not that the moon watches two lovers through the night, but that he watches a young girl cry herself to sleep. Maybe it is for these reasons, they aren't so alone; they can watch society face their own loneliness and heartbreak as they face theirs. The sun so bright, so joyous, calm, and hopeful, the moon so mysterious and beautiful, but how sad they must be.

7

As continuous nights have passed and a series of suns have risen, I realize I have forgotten to keep you up to date, so allow me to inform you of my recent endeavors. I had dedicated the first day in the cycle of my neglect of offering you my story to finishing the stairs; it was in finishing them that I moved on to the top floor, which wasn't nearly as large as the first. Thank the Lord. I needed to get the house cleaned because I knew if I didn't do it soon enough, I would have become infected with lung cancer. Of course, once I had cleaned, I could paint the horrid mess of the walls. This mess thankfully was mainly confined to the first floor. I did, in fact, recognize prior to the activity that painting is a process, and so for the process to be complete before my belonging's arrival, I must have begun promptly. So, I finished the stairs, cleaning the arm rail and every crease between the steps, and for those next four days, succeeding the one I have just described, I moved every piece of furniture to the center of each room using the sheets that were covering the fixtures to line the floors.

The act of painting had caused me to feel like a lab rat in a maze in those four days that I worked from the rising sun to the near rise of the moon, ending my days completely exhausted and completely covered in paint, but I had somehow managed to paint the kitchen, the study, and the foyer. Alas, only missing the dining room, hallways, stairs, and of course, the entirety of the top floor. Wonderful. How can you feel so accomplished one moment and so miserable the next? Those four days, I covered the blue, gold, and purple walls with white paint, but on that fourth day, I had drained those metal buckets of every last drop, and so on that fifth day, I had to face what I had been dreading, meeting that most awkward man once again. Truly, I must blame myself for this. I am most peculiar in my meticulous opinions of people. It is for this reason that I have only a few friends, and I still cannot yet find attributes in my parents to which I enjoy. I find many people quite bothersome; this man is just another to fill the list. This fifth day came, and I hastily entered his store with my head down, purchasing my paint, and with an even quicker pace, I managed an escape. My walk home this time was much less philosophical. The cans of paint were large and heavy. Since my venture was in the midday and not at the top of the morning, I was stopped by five inhabitants of the town, each approaching me with such hospitality, the men offering to help but only with slight insult asking me if I was capable of manual labor and following with the similarly insinuating question, "You don't paint in those clothes, right?" The women, much kinder but even more annoying. I presume, because of my slight accent and my dress, they are all simply in awe. I had not a partner in my life promising at first sight how devoted they should be to me, yet I had never step foot onto the streets of smalltown Georgia before. I can't recollect how I managed an escape. On this walk, I did happen to come to another realization: people of the South seem to manage to be the kindest and happiest of people, all the while deeply insulting or annoying you. Masters of subjacent speech, I suppose. This is in contrast to the North; northern inhabitants simply say what they think regardless of your emotions and most definitely not with a smile. This new life has not only given me a new type of work experience but a new education as well. Finally, this gruesome walk fell to an end as I reached my still-broken mailbox, and in reaching my home, every annoyance I had met on this day vanished at the sight of the willows. I walked down that grey path once again in peace, comforted by the willow trees kindled in the rays of the sun. I got to my porch; a porch with only a slight hue of white paint on a dark withered wood, a railing that looks as though it wished to be the Leaning Tower of Pisa, and a bird's nest above the door in a support beam. To complete the porch— there are three steps one walks up to reach my front door, one, two, three. This day, having made it up the steps, I placed my right foot on the porch, then left, and again my right, but the damned house had decided that the two planks beneath me should break right in their center, yielding my foot into their jaws and further into the porch's abyss. My foot, having been clenched by the jaws, unable to move, forced me to awkwardly hop onto my left foot in avoidance of falling over, then stabilize my left foot and place the buckets of paint at the foot of the door. I grabbed my right leg and the door, pulling on my leg while pushing on the door, and alas, my leg was unleashed with not a drop of blood drawn by that porch's vicious bite. This event led me to the conclusion that my porch was not able to support itself; therefore, it can most definitely not support another. I, once so eager to finish my painting in preparation for my belongings; I, so prepared, so planned. I, then dumbfounded in search of a new plan.

The following three days surpassing this event, I had painted my bedroom and the upstairs hall. The rooms below left unfinished I decided shall simply be a project for the future. There, that is all.

8

It is only my tenth day in this house, and I feel as if this is all just a vacation, a short trip to enjoy a new type of work, but one that will end soon. I feel that my aunt is still waiting in her white rocker on her porch, glancing off into a distant point on the sea over the harbor, waiting for me to return to her. I only wish this was true. There is a poison in the southern air which has a way of shaping itself into what it wishes; horrid or wondrous. I am today again walking to Main Street, this time to the general store, of course, all for what will go into the porch's fortuitous repairs. The time, 7:23 am, early morning to avoid all life in this town. Though in contrast to my last visits to Main Street, I had to plan to be transported back to my home by truck. My first ride in this town, despite what most may say about the event, this being that the man, my driver was quite delightful, simply talkative. I, of course, found him to be annoying and the ride to be agonizing. However, in relation to my other visits to Main

Street, I was not looking forward to the activity, but I have no ability to negate the visit because it is much needed. So, in the positive light of things, by making this trip and returning by truck with one of the townsmen, I will be able to bring home a much larger heap of supplies, forgoing my future visits for a good amount of time. Therefore, regardless of my expectations, I must greet today's driver with a smile and keep the thought in mind that I will not have to make this trip for days upon my luck.

The general store is much larger than that man's shop, the most awkward man, of course, who is just down the road. This store is the size of a Woolworths but embellished with the most rustic tools and lined from floor to ceiling with small drawers on the remaining walls which are filled with all kinds of metallic shapes. The store is far from any I have experienced; dark, confederate, and foundering, but it does have all the equipment I will need. I should not be pessimistic considering the prices of goods; the South has made me into a millionaire, so it seems. The woman running the store who I may say is very large with manly shoulders and fried hair but with the softest of temperament (quite deceiving she is) was forced to help poor me and was quick to do so, most certainly due to the fact the words 'inexperienced,' 'city,' and 'man' oozed out of the sweat perspiring from my brow just in the looking at the thousands of nails, although, I like to tell myself she came to my aid simply because I was the only customer in the store. I find myself now to have spent two and a half hours in this store, two and a half hours of my day, of my life, gone and all because of the complexity of wood and nails. After this most unfavorable two and a half hours, I discover now the woman's husband is the one to drive me home in his pickup truck. A funny idea it is, a pickup truck since before I had nothing to pick up. This man, I do not mind. He too, is large like his wife, blunt, not one to smile, yet entirely respectful; therefore, someone I could find myself getting along with.

The ride, despite my pre-resignations was quite pleasant; he, Stewart, even helped me unload with only minimal commentary while doing so. A simple one-line, "This is a heck of a house." And upon finishing unloading, "Well, I wish you the best of luck, and if you need anything, you know where to find me." I asked if he would want a few dollars in return, "Oh no," he replied.

"Well, Stewart, very nice to meet you and quite nice of you to help; I should see you soon. Good day." I say to him in return.

Yes, I, William Hathaway, could return an ounce of kindness in conversation regardless of your probably wretched opinion of me.

Now, as I watch Stewart drive away, I realize I do not feel as alone. His leaving is a beautiful scene. Beginning with the bottom of the steps attached to the porch, then through those weeping willows on each side of the long grey drive, his truck rumbling in the center between the trees with a perfect beam of sun through a branch reflecting off the tailgate. The artist inside my mind had already painted a portrait of the scene by the time he had faded away into the distance. I think to myself, if only everyone could leave a fragile person in such a beautiful way, so many hearts could be saved. Or is it that I am only now seeing the beauty in absence?

I walk up those three steps onto my porch, looking into the hole which had consumed my foot just previously. How was I to fix this atrocity one may wonder; why, yes, I too wonder. Knowing myself and my simple struggles in painting a room, what was I to do on matters of construction? The only construction I have taken part in is the construction of a court case. Putting my lack of experience aside, I have talked in depth to that kind, general store-owning couple in my two and a half hours in their presence, and I have read a book on the matter which I believe constitutes the ability to take apart a rotting porch and hammer on new boards to already standing support beams.

9

This day, not terrible in the slightest, but long. I am not so ready to slide on a pair of gloves and begin working on the porch's wooden repairs, so I grab a broom and begin carefully sweeping the porch instead. As much as I had surveyed the home, inch by inch, analyzing its attributes, I had not even explored the porch. I presume this is because I had seen it; I saw it every time I walked up my driveway or got near a window on the first floor, and so the need to experience the porch in all of its glory through walking upon it, was not a need that crossed my mind or one that caused my body to tingle in the lack of doing so. Furthermore, in being horrified by the porch's teeth in the trauma of its caving, I find myself in a bit of a conundrum in an attempt to clean it. I devise a plan; I take my broom, reach its end out and slam it down onto a portion of the porch, then once the test is passed, I place one foot onto the examined portion and press down, letting almost all of my body mass onto that size twelve shoe, and once the second portion of the test is marked complete, I move forward and sweep. I realize if anyone was to be near to witness, they would be immediately battered by laughter or confusion, followed by a possible worry for my sanity. This does not matter because the South is incredible at keeping people away from one another (at times). Alas, arriving at the final portion of the porch, a clap of thunder rings, and a cascade of rain begins to fall from the sky. Here I find myself now jumping to and from each designated 'safe spot' among the random locations of the porch in order to avoid another teething incident, just managing to escape the rain. I rush inside, now closing every window upstairs that the rain had just begun to pour through. I save my bedroom from the rain although only momentarily before endangering my lungs in the immediate intoxication of paint fumes. I had not closed the windows even for a second after the application of the paint, and so I realize now how sickening the smell is. I flee downstairs to my soon-to-be study where I had hoped to simply spend my afternoon sitting and reading, but in my arrival to the study, I find myself making acquittance to the immense pile of furniture covered in white sheets in the center of the room. I did not mean to be met with a model of Mount Everest in my reading room, although the mess is quite the perfect display, and I physically cannot work outside; therefore, I am confined to the indoors, and with the paint dry I can unveil the mountain and finally set up this room. Ah, yes, how productive of a thought.

An hour later now, and I have since managed the unveiling and a plan that should be quicker to execute than the time it took to draw up, exceptionally grateful for the precursor of this home's lack of interest in their furniture for he or she left this room alone with a large bookshelf, a Chesterfield, a sitting table, a beautifully crafted wooden chair, and most exciting of all, to match the chair, a handcrafted wooden desk with every centimeter perfectly fitted with a wooden embedded design, brass corner accents, drawers with matching brass handles, and an upper level with a secret compartment hidden behind another unique design. Oh, how I love anything stationary or related.

Upon the completion of my study's transformation, the rain still falls from the sky, and so the time has come, and I finally receive the ability to read peacefully as I had planned nearly three hours ago to do. Laying upon this Chesterfield, I escape this world only to enter that of a Russian nobleman. My mission tonight, to save a girl of hard labor in Siberia (you should find I am referring to the work of Leo Tolstoy's Resurrection). I work to defeat a new type of legal system, how I find the law so intriguing. If only my young protagonist would portray the legal system in all its glory, for I find it quite lacking through his portrayal.

10

Zzzzz... Zzzzzz...... Zzzzzz..... I open my eyes to directly face the most disgusting of a creature—a fly. Immediately swatting the little demon away, now awake, I place my book on its newly stationed shelf, looking out the window to find the sun has already risen. Though still in a state of sleep, just now beginning to see clearly, I trudge myself room by room to find my pocket watch; with no trace, I face those stairs and somehow reach my bedroom where of course, the silver pocket watch reflects the sun's rays to blind me in my entry. If only it was animate, I am positive it would be laughing at the sight of me. Opening the humored watch, I catch my first glimpse of the time today, 10:37 am. 10:37! How could I have slept to this hour? This was an hour that I had not reached in sleep since my time as a young boy when I had pneumonia while still living in Nottingham. Was I sick? No, of course not. Well, being there is no time to waste, I shall move on into my day and onto productivity.

My day has since consisted of waiting for the porch and yard to dry, leaving myself inside, where I continue to paint. Ending my day earlier than usual to read once again, only this time, making it to the bed before shutting my eyes. Here I lay in this hard bed, holding a book I have already read, thinking, "Oh, how I wish for my belongings to arrive." This night, I put myself into bed quite early in hopes of avoiding the abstruse awakening I experienced this morning. So, dear reader, I wish you a good night.

11

As I mentioned only nine hours ago, I had wished for my belongings to arrive, and every morning is a reassurance of this. Not a single curtain is to be found in this large house, not a single curtain to be draped onto the perfectly large windows that decorate my bedroom walls. Yes, I have had the opportunity to purchase drapes, but if you have not collected, I am a frugal man. I do not have a very need to be frugal; it is simply a desire that has framed my way of life. And so, it is for this reason, and for the reason that I have my own drapes which block the sun's rays so nicely on their way to me. There, back to the thought, the sun's rays! Though so beautiful, with their colors of yellow and orange, how bright they shine in the morning. Rethinking, I do not believe I have the right to complain as someone should not have the ability to curse an item of their praise. Thou shall not hate such a deadly beauty but embrace. And embrace I shall. Now awake, I can move down to my kitchen, sit at those glass doors, and read.

Alas, I find myself, already forty-five minutes later, the sun finally well above the trees and my book well-read. May I leave this large table's side and eat a small meal? I may assure you, due to my visit to that kind man Stewart's store, I was able to stock my shelves more heavily, and I am to have a refrigerator installed. As, I had also, in that trip to Stewart's, placed my order; only to find this most necessary box is to arrive in nearly three weeks, quite astounding, but at least it will be on its way and that is all I can do. I might as well not dwell on something I have no further control over. Done with my meal, I make my way to the bedroom yet again to dress and prepare for this day of work ahead of me. I wrestle through my smallest suitcase to find my most worn-out trousers. I had hoped to find a pair of overalls, but I caught a glimpse of myself in the mirror and laughed at the thought that I may own a pair of denim pants. Today, the earth is hot, so on top of those light, grass-stained working trousers, I button on my most sheer shirt over an undershirt, and I'm off onto another hunt, a common one—the search for shoes. With limited supplies, a pair of loafers appears to be the best I can do. I do assure you, these loafers are already muddy and worn, much like my pants, and very thick, large overall, less loafer, more clog or even boot-like if I may; if a boot were built to be cut below the ankle. Descending these stairs, I face the task of collecting my supplies, so I plan along the way, mentally preparing myself for the labor I am to undertake momentarily. This internal event went about as follows,

'William, you are about to put together a porch. Yes, a porch. You are going to fix a large southern porch with your own hands, your own ten fingers. So, you will start at the hole, yes. Then you will take off the planks. Ok. And you will place your new, pre-cut planks onto the porch. Should you stain the planks before? No. No, after. Ok, then you will repeat this process. All will be well. Yes, yes, all truly will be quite well. William, if you can prove a murderer guilty in a court of law, you can build a porch.'

With the scrambling and insanity playing out in the space between the foyer and kitchen, I can declare myself primed for the task. I stand twenty feet from the front door hiding half of my body behind the wall of the kitchen, staring at that doorknob. I make my way. First, my left foot moves my body around the corner wall, then my right progresses me further to the handle, and then what feels as if one hundred hours have passed in one minute, I arrive at the door facing the window, through the door, looking out to the drive and to the willows. My right hand jolts in an attempt to grasp the knob, with a handle, I twist, and it opens, and I look to the hole, and now, the work begins.

12

What can I say about a porch? Well, three hours and forty-five minutes, three splinters, and a length of odd discoveries intertwined with pounds of leaves and twigs removed, and I have only unlatched fourteen planks, every plank exactly six inches in width and sixty in length. Fourteen planks, not even half the number which encompasses the porch on the front of the house. How I wish I'd never started this project. I must go inside just to sit, to eat, to drink the Nile. I believe considering the labor I have undergone in these weeks, I have worked arduously, I have worked for preposterous lengths, non-stop so it feels. Considering the heat and the vigor of the activities I have partaken, you would believe me to be falling down in my step, sweating like a dog as the young people say, oh and possibly quite 'pooped,' as they may say as well. Still, you must believe me when I tell you, I am not any of these things; I'm completely invigorated, awake, and indifferent to the work. I must truly have gone mad on the train ride from Maine, as I only take thirty minutes to pause and then I am on my feet once more and out the door. I decided, though, because it was noon, that instead of resuming the process of unlatching boards, I should begin attaching them. I decided this to be a good plan considering that if I continue the process of unlatching, I should have no proficient way to enter my home. To put into perspective, the porch's state is to be explained; you see facing the house, I have in the center, two large doors, then to the left and right, a large window on each side. If you remember that tragic incident of my foot entangling with the wrath of the wood, then you may remember it was my right foot that was placed to the right of the front door. Therefore, the fourteen planks removed stretch from the hinges of that right door where the plank of which the hole is situated to the farthest right corner of the porch. To articulate my plan, I am to begin attaching planks so that I will still have the left side of the porch, at the bare minimum, for my use. Now, without any further rambling, I must return to the porch's floor; setting up on those leftward, still-standing planks, I pick up my first board, which feels heavier than those I was just removing (I believe this to be a good sign). I then place it down with utmost accuracy to ensure no mistake or worse a reoccurrence of this event. With my board of oak happily situated, I take my first nail, hold it over its pre-calculated destination, raise my hammer, and with a squint of my eye—bang! The nail latches to the wood with just one swing. Oh, how even more exhilarating this makes the process! Again and again, I swing four times, and finally, each nail I had placed has vanished into the boards for what I wish to be for forever or at least for the rest of the time which I shall spend in this home. Corner by corner, nail by nail, swing by swing, the exhilaration has since transformed into indifference. Three boards and I return inside to swallow a bit of that river, examine my cabinets, etcetera, etcetera. With this break well extended, I pull on those no longer fresh gloves, gloves which make me feel so rugged; the brown leather amongst my warm ivory skin to match my eyes. With the gloves on my hands, I carry out four more planks in two trips and set them near my empty hole. One last trip inside for water, of course, and out again onto my knees. The grass stains on my knees this morning had turned more to a shade of brown and were almost lost in all entirety, though I find this to be quite good as brown compliments my complexion and my current state much nicer than the previous shade of green. Eighteen nails, three boards, and sixty inches down, I travel to place the first nails on the fourth plank, sliding forward onto my left knee, which, when implanted, implants a rip into my trousers, the skin exposed as a result and torn along with it. I find a splinter hidden within a bed of blood. The bigger annoyance being the fact that I must take further time away from my construction when I have just begun working again. I drag myself inside, into the kitchen, then with no luck, to my bedroom. With hope fading, I rummage through my belongings for longer than I have been working just now. Finally, a bandage at last! Blood still falling (only intensifying my ruggedness), I step into the bathroom to clean the wound; removing yet again another splinter, I apply the bandage. At last, I may return again. I have decided to keep my pants, though ripped, on my body. It appears, honestly, that I have no other option.

More gracefully than before, I collapse to my knees, and there, the fifth plank attached. No longer sliding forward, I step upward to each nail and swing. In contrast to that metal clang, a voice, a feminine, angelic voice, "Someone did move into that old Manor!" The voice rings with such a delight as if the possessor of such a voice had won a bet to explain such glee, and so interrupting my work once again, I look across my yard to the voice that has directed itself at me. I look across my yard, away from my work, only for my heart to be stopped and then to soar as if it were leaving me entirely and flying straight through the clouds as if to meet its Lord. I stand on this porch with no voice, no movement; she has immediately possessed every inch of me alone in her gaze. And there she stands, holding onto the knob of the door she has just closed, her left leg awkwardly positioned over her right, just nearly crossing, one sock higher than the other, a shoelace untied. Just a second has passed, and her skirt floats slightly upward in the wind. Finally, she takes her hand off that knob to protect her decency then, in just another sweep, she places her hair behind her ear. Her hair, oh, her hair! Having the sun as her accomplice, it shines so perfectly to light up the strawberry within the blonde. The wind—another friend—blowing the strands of gold just right as if she brought the breeze herself. Her face— glowing, so dewy, perfectly sculpted, her lips parted, her eyes so blue, so bright I can see the sea. In just one gaze, she possessed me, and in just one blink, she has configured my mind into the belief there is no other soul as perfect. So, there she stands as a pearl statue of Aphrodite, and so the wind blows, and she is a dove soaring through cotton clouds, then she blinks and a hurricane rains upon the re-opening of her eyes, and she smiles and the gates of Heaven open, and then she speaks once more. Why should she speak, for I am only a man, and she is not of this world but a goddess trapped inside it? But alas, the goddess speaks, "Hey there mister!" Within this one line, the world which she should not belong to stops; the willow's branches pause mid-swing, the wind does not blow, the birds are unable to move, the grass halts its swaying at the angle of the wind, and it is only her and I. The world stopped— my heart with it. With her words, she has shot me with a bullet of euphoria which holds my chest inward and causes my breath to escape me, for when it returns, I can only smile so greatly so widely as if I was a child who had just returned to his mother after a long time away. My eyes gleam, and all I can say in return, "Hello." I have never been so compelled by any being in my life's entirety, but her immediate possession of me, body and mind, she must have known that in the simple act of greeting a man, she holds his soul in her hands.

Still with a marvelous gleam, "Oh Sir, where are you from?"

"Well, I have just escaped Maine."

"And that's an accent from a Maine-lander?" she says in obvious hopes for the answer to my slight English accent which I believe breaks through to southerners.

"Oh no, my dear, not Maine, Nottingham." To be so astonished and now speak as I have known her for years. My dear?

"Oh well, my fine Sir, I must enlighten you, I have always dreamed of visiting the UK."

Even in her mockery, she maintains sincerity.

All of a sudden, a loud voice, "Charlotte, you are going to be late if you don't get off that porch!"

"Oh, goodbye!" she chants.

"Goodbye." I almost burst too loud, just in order for her to hear.

Then in a matter of seconds, my most beautiful sight is gone, vanishing to the mist behind the willows, as all I am left to do is stand still on that new plank in complete eumoiriety. What is there to do but replay her words, her smile, her sparkling eyes, over and over without end? Has the love of my life just left me? Will I ever see her again? I know her name, but will she ever know mine? Regardless, I know that if I do not get to hold her or laugh with her or let alone speak to her ever again in this life, I have been made fully complete. The moment from her sitting, partially frowning face to her smile, this moment, she draws it out; she does not look up, that is until, when she does, she takes in what she has seen then this is when her lips begin to widen to a closed grin, then to an opening, and her teeth may finally appear. Here she has almost reached her most precious state, but behind the revealing of her teeth, her eyes finally catch up, and they smile larger than her lips and teeth ever could. This moment will forever be engraved in my mind, for it shall not ever leave me, not on earth or in any eternity. I realize I am complete, but how am I to live without her? Since her goodbye, I have only stared neverendingly at where she once stood, looking into her absent eyes, minutes have passed, and still, I cannot move. Was my Aphrodite really a Medusa? Have I been frozen in time? I have to lift my foot just to see. I move inside as if these were my first steps taken on earth. William, what is happening? I've never realized I could feel so strongly for any being on this earth, not my family, my friends, or even a young love long ago. Was this Charlotte even real? Am I still on this earth, had I died in this house, or had I fallen into a coma in Maine, and is this all but a dream? I just... I do not know. For the first time in my livelihood, I am without words. This young girl has drained all intellect from me. She really has stolen everything: my heart, my soul, and my mind! Charlotte, please return! What am I to do? I must force myself to return, anchor myself, and sink back into reality. With my mouth still open, my heart still stopped, and my brain overwhelmed by everything and nothing at once, I open the knob and once again go out to work, just as I had before the encounter. It is just too strange; the fact that in my wake, in my work, I had no idea, no inkling that my life, my sad, lonely life would be altered, changed entirely, ruined, and fulfilled by one young Charlotte. I finally return to my hammering and aiding to the porch. At last, the sixth board placed, now onto the seventh.

Oh, but my reader, did I mention my Charlotte, the little goddess, does not but look over the age of seventeen.

13

What is a man to do? What could he have possibly done? I must continue my day, proceed to nail and hammer these boards, shower, and retire to my study, all in ecstasy. In order to cope with the gain and loss of the love of my life, I go about as if the whole opera did not even occur. It is not until now, sitting here in my study, reading another Russian novelist's work, drowning in the ocean of what seems to be never-ending words, that I am struck once more by the passion and eumoiriety. I sit on this Chesterfield, no longer reading but once again replaying her words; I smile. I have spent this whole day without being held by the grip of her powers in absence of her spell, but as soon as the work comes to a halt, her spell activates itself once more, twisting and wiggling itself through my nerves into the fibers of my brain. I sit as a monument for the evening, replaying the scene of the day, that is, until the terribly wrenching voice of the man, the one who sent her off the porch, comes about again like a broken record. Although, this harsh, loud, obnoxious voice allows me to break myself free and walk myself upstairs. Maybe sleep shall draw me into an empty abyss away from her vicious hold.

How mistaken I have found myself to be; my night filled with only dreams of her ivory face, her peach lips, her strawberry yet golden hair, her silhouette, and her heavenly voice. Only in my dreams have I found her touch to be more fulfilling than her words and her lips to be as soft as they appear. My little goddess is truly a little demon in disguise. Will I ever rid myself of this longing, or am I forever forsaken?

14

The morning came, and I, as normal, rose with the sun. I do not imagine her face or internally speak her name; I go on as if yesterday and as if she ceased to exist. I get dressed, and I walk myself down those steps through an abnormal path, not through the foyer or even the study, but I walk through the sitting room into the dining room, then down the hall, and at last to the kitchen. With an unusual spring to my step, I jolt into my pantry amongst the cabinetry, fix myself a fine meal, and set it at my large table. Oh, but wait! I leave this table to my study to retrieve my book. Alright, back to my meal now with a book, and well, I eat. There is nothing more really. Finishing this sacramental feeling routine— the plate and cup washed, my stomach satisfied, and my book back peacefully on its shelf. In the act of placing my book on its high shelf, I realize with the lift of my hand my watch is not attached as it usually is; with a sigh, I know I must climb that large staircase to retrieve it. My home in Maine had two levels but short ceilings, therefore fewer stairs. I feel I may cause you to believe I am a man out of shape, fat dragging, but I promise you, I am not, quite the opposite you see, I am not exceptionally lazy, though maybe not the most muscular, but I'm not anywhere near large, instead tall and quite slender. Let me tell you this to postulate my appearance. This is a subject I rather not leave to the imagination. Maybe you recall my pocket watch's normal hiding place, on the window seal to the left of my bed. Well, today, it appears it is not here; therefore, I am forced to actually hunt for the object. Picking up every shoe and article of clothing on the ground, shaking my pillows and sheets, nothing. I move my search to the bathroom. Aha! At last, the search is over just in the entrance of this secondary seeking point. Yanking the watch off the sink and into the air almost at eye level, praising its return to me, my victory receives interruption by a knock at my door. The knocker not knocking harshly but still managing an echo through the halls. A knock on my door! Well, this hasn't happened since May. I hop out of that bathroom, letting the watch fall out of my hands as I hastily run down those steps as if I was a child who had just been invited out to the candy store. Mid staircase, I land on a step in order to stop this haste, straighten myself into the man I am, and walk with not an ounce of desire down the remainder of those steps, regaining my dignity.

With an opening of the door, "Hi, Sir!"

A second one of her bullets hit me, and I am completely stopped again; how can this be reality?

She apparently noticed my lack of movement or breath as she adds, "Good morning!"

"Oh. Yes, yes, a good morning to you." I force myself to reply, and more forcefully, I hide my astoundment.

"Oh, I am sorry it is early, but you see, after yesterday and my abrupt departure, I kept thinking about you all day, and so I got myself up and over to you... to formally introduce myself... Hi." she says again before introducing herself, "I'm Charlotte."

She, my little beauty, was thinking of me. Of me, of I? This must be the third bullet!

In complete joy, I respond, "Hello Charlotte, I am William. It is quite a pleasure to formally meet you."

"Oh, I could listen to you say my name all day!"

"I assure you I would be happy to speak it, but currently, I'm a little flooded. I am afraid a hammer may drown out my voice."

She laughs, and as I attempt to keep my smile average, my eyes, they remain uncontrolled, gleaming foolishly, I presume.

She continues, "Speaking of a hammer, I just wanted to introduce myself and let you know that if you need any help, I would love to be of service." Before I could speak, she interrupts, "Really, school is out, and my parents are too exhausting to be around."

She sounds so eager to insert herself into my presence.

"Well, truly, that would be greatly appreciated, I must get this porch done before my things arrive, and it seems I am running out of time."

I do not know if she was expecting my answer to be a yes, but regardless she replies, "Oh, how grand! Are you working today?"

"I am indeed."

"Well then, consider me yours!"

A fourth bullet. Unimaginable and maybe not in the way she intended, I do so consider her mine.

"Sounds great. Although, I just dropped my watch before you arrived; let me fetch it, and we shall start." I say almost questionably.

Entering my home, I, already up three steps, hear from below, "Oh wow. This house is huge!"

She followed me in! To tell you, I do not know what I was expecting; she simply followed me in. How brave, how she felt us so close, so soon.

"It is quite large," I smile.

"And you live here alone?"

"Oh yes. It is just me," I smirk to myself, she, completely unbeknownst to my internal fascination with her meaning behind such a question.

"Huh." her only response.

Huh? What could this mean? What was her motive in this slight exhale of breath, this 'huh?' Does she think me some widow, does she think me a weirdo, or does she think of my availability, of my heart's openness to her own?

"Ah yes, here it is." I divert any attention to these confounding questions back to the watch.

I turn around, and there she is in the door frame of my bedroom; I smile once more. She runs to the window where my pocket watch normally situates itself.

"This view, this yard! It is so crazy, I live only next door, yet your yard is much more serene."

"When I moved in, its tranquility was the only thing keeping me sane."

At this moment, her hands lie holding the window seal while her face leans so close to the glass as I remain quite closely behind her, looking out over her shoulder; she looks up to me, staring for a moment, forcing me to await the arrival of her nymphetic grin. A fifth bullet of euphoria she shoots; when shall she decide such pain is enough? The way she looks to me as if directly into my mind, as though she is reading it, the way she smiles; her company is none other than an ineffable feeling of solitude.

"Would you like a tour?" I ask her.

"Would I!" she replies with the utmost positivity.

By now, I have absolutely no recollection of life before Charlotte; I walk her through my home. With every room, she pauses, she scans, and feels a piece of furniture until she decides she has seen enough, and we move on. With each room, she paints a new scene with each of her special pieces of commentary. Only in reaching the study she lets out a small gasp and the largest of a smile. "Look at these books!"

I, caught off guard respond, "Oh, you like to read; why those on the shelf are only a few of mine, the rest are coming soon, I should hope."

"I love to read! If only my parents found the same value in books. If they did, I would have read every book written."

"You can help me unload them when they arrive and then read any of your choosing."

She interrupts, "How do you know I will be back?"

In consternation at this remark, I flee to my worries, had I said something wrong? Did I stumble too close? Does she not find me attractive?

Before I can think up a response, she laughs, "Oh my... you really do want me back, and of course, I will be. Nothing to fret about."

Maybe she really is reading my mind when she stared at me as she does. I simply tell her that I am glad she will come back to help and that I enjoy her company. Although, I quickly make an attempt to proceed us along.

During our time on the porch, I spent much of it nailing and hammering while she worked on taking out those old boards. Yet in all this time, not hardly a moment together was overthrown by silence. Four hours it is that she spent with me today and four hours it is that we spoke. Our talks mostly focused first on books, then on my profession, and her hopes for her future which she is not entirely sure of, only she knows she wants to be important, high class, needed, and helpful. I, of course, attempted to sway her to law or politics, which she declared as completely valid options, nodding her head in confirmation. Silence only fell when one or both of us were in a state of complete concentration. The morning she had arrived in long faded, and with its disappearance, it had become mid-afternoon; that is, the time has now come for my darling to leave. My offer to walk her home, she refuses, and so I instead settle and walk her to the porch steps. Off the steps, she races down, walking to the left, then across the field. I walk to the end of this newly built porch, leaning onto a column; in my incandescent joy, I watch her walk away. Almost halfway across the field, she stops mid-leap to turn and wave with that nymphetic gleam once more. I wave just long enough for my hand to be touched by gravity, falling just far enough to catch my heart as if to slow its pace.

I whisper, "Goodbye, my love. Goodbye, my Charlotte."

And just like that, my day continues, yet unlike before, there is not a constant longing for her or thought of her. I am able to continue living. The continuous thought of Charlotte has morphed into a much healthier obsession. Just in the hours we spent together for I no longer have a need to meet her again, to introduce myself, or to have her near me. The feeling, now, as if we had lived our entire lives side by side as if she was completely mine, and I, hers. The worry of if she thinks of me or if we shall see each other again has been fulfilled. Instead of that bewitching, maddening, longing obsession, I may now live with only ardent joy. At last, I am released; the knowledge of her thought of me lets me know I am not mad, that she feels the same as I. We long for each other; it is a redamancy, and for that, I may live again.

Charlotte returned to her home with the promise she would return to me tomorrow, to which I assured her it would be much more pleasant of a day with her in my company. Left to myself, I continue with my hammering and adding of planks until finally upon the sixth hour of my workday, my front porch reaches completion. The last side of the porch, if you care to know, would be done at a later date after the arrival and unpacking of my things (the event Charlotte has already scheduled to attend). Being such a task I have just completed, I reward myself this evening with a heftier meal than normal, a book, and an early rest. Rest filled with dreams of my lovely, young Charlotte as she smiles and dances in fields of daisies whilst directing her smile, her eyes, and body to me. Holding my heart, I could sense the biggest smile ever to dare mount my face. In a scene in which the yellow sun colors the fog, within the petrichor, she jumps, and with a fallen angel of a look, she runs to me; before she reaches me, I shake my head, knowing I am without any option but to catch my dearest darling. Purposefully placing us on the soft, green grass, she rolls over me, allowing her head to levitate over mine, her eyes only inches away, her lips even closer; she knows the power she holds as she lowers herself onto me. With a smile, she leans in. The tease she is. She does not follow through but turns to my ear to whisper. What does she whisper? The sun that framed my angel's face, shown through more than my sleeping mind, outstretching its wicked arms, I find myself awake, taken away from my heaven. I must withhold my anger for the person, who is more than anything I could have ever rewarded myself with in such a dream, is to be walking through my very doors in only a matter of hours.

Dreams are indeed so kind. They take us away from our wicked world and into our greatest desires, a perfect play, and we are cast as the stars. Dreams release us from the nightmares we live, only now my world has turned itself into a dream and I must not mix my new reality with the false. Charlotte, my nymphet, my feverish angel, a master at persuading strangers that they had known her for all of life known to man. She does not realize she falsely sanctifies a man's unholy love. Only one day in proximity, one day enough to breathe her breath, and I have already betrothed herself to mine.

15

This day, one so easy to begin for not any thought of mine within it, may be better. Without a need to leave my bed or even arise so early, I have found simply a joyous will to live. Although I may wish to lay in dreams of my dear, she is to come, and with that I must get up and about. I dart out of bed to dress and eat. I look out my glass doors to admire the world's serenity and the beauty which follows. I complete, step by step, this routine which I have followed for all my weeks in this home, yet with every step once planned, once so ordinary, nearly feeling as though it were a duty, I find now colorful, now fulfilling. My world seems as if as soon as Charlotte stepped onto my porch, the grey and lonely cloud, which hung just above me, was blown away as she spoke, and just as she smiled, the sun arrived as that cloud's replacement.

I begin to get out of my chair by the doors in the kitchen and make my way outside, and I notice each step I take is no longer followed by the sound of a foot meeting a hard, wooden ground but with a lightness; my walk I take in ecstasy, my floor gone entirely, replaced by a cotton cloud. How is that, my doorknob not so cold?

Opening the front door, "Charlotte."

"Hi! Am I too early?" she questions worriedly of the possibility of her mistake.

"You could never be too early."

"Well then, what's the task for today?"

"Staining the wood of what is done of the porch."

It amazes me; with every word she speaks, she never ceases to smile. For if her teeth are not shown, then her lips are curved, or at the least, a small, attempting dimple takes way at her cheek. Or perhaps, besides any of those things, always, in every moment, no matter the time, her eyes hold a specific gleam; a gleam in which, if it could speak, I only imagine it may say, "You make me complete, you are all I live for, all I breathe for, and I will do all a gleam can do to persuade you to love me." This gleam is part of the posterity that our ' relationship' is a redamancy. Though you may wish for me to finish, I must go on to tell you that this gleam, so beautiful and wonderful, is nearly annoying for it is driving me to a strange madness. Her eyes make me feel as if I am instead the only man on this earth. No, far better, as if I am the only man to be of any good looks, character, or of ability to walk, to talk, because there are still thousands of men, all completely wretched in all aspects of which she does not love. With this, it is not that she chooses me by the force of there only being myself as her singular option, but rather as the testimony to myself exceeding that of any other living being. It all makes me wonder whether the world still spins, why I have been the one to be chosen, how have I been crowned the king of her magnificent kingdom?

Working another day, staining each board and talking endlessly; how conversation between us flows so neverendingly, I myself still unsure. Today she has asked me more about the law and about Maine. What the city was like, my life which seems long faded. She has brought me back to my boyhood on the streets of Nottingham, and while we talk relentlessly of myself, she shudders at the idea of discussing her own life. She discusses the town, who is who, the neighbor's quirks, the best store for eating, for candy, for books, even of school, only occasionally she speaks of a friend or two, but never of her own parents, childhood, current fascinations, none of that. Maybe this was all just another piece to her perfect puzzle, how she is so delightful and engaging, for she does not overcast regardless of what ease it would be. Feeling as if only twenty minutes had passed, two and a half hours had been, and at this mark Charlotte and I meet in the middle of the porch, both finished staining each of our sides. I, completely focused, somehow unnoticing of her near to me. She turns, whipping her skirt around, sliding on her knees just far enough for her forehead to reach my own, to which I look up swiftly, "We are done!" She smiles. This time only three inches from that of my own smile. Before I may get up, she does so before me. In this moment, I am sure she knows she holds my body in her hands as she springs up, practically hitting my face with her skirt, allowing my eyes to be placed underneath. I look to the porch quicker than light, in the feeling of invasion, and in hopes, she will believe I have not fallen victim to her trick. At last, I follow in pursuit of her, rising onto my feet. "Hurry! Get off, get off!" she yells, pushing me down the steps with one hand on my back, her other quite lower, below my waist; she follows, "That was close!"

I stand laughing, "What was close?"

"Well, we have just stained it, haven't we?"

"Ah, yes. I see."

"Hm, yes, yes…" she says, mocking my outwitted tone. "So, you can't be on it; it will leave a mark or pick up bits of the stain or something." she informs me.

"I see your most valid point." I contend.

We both stand in my drive right below the steps looking peculiarly at the sky, and I, just as a branch of a tree, interrupt our observations, "What shall we do?"

She snaps, "What do you mean, what shall we do?"

"Well, I was going to take you inside. I've made up a picnic, and I thought we may make this workday a bit more pleasant."

Any sort of annoyance seemed to have left her, "You made us a picnic?"

I was worried she might think me insane, but alas, she interrupts, "That is so sweet of you. Wow, that really is just grand that you would do that for me!"

"Well, of course I did, but the problem is, it seems to be trapped inside."

Her eyes turn from softness to confusion, "Then we should go get it."

"Yes, yes, but you see we can't step on the stain."

"You mean to tell me with this big house, this is the only door?"

"No, there is a door in the back."

"So, we should go through it then." she speaks as though to insult my intelligence as if she thought lesser of me; this could not be allowed,

"Listen, while yes, there are other options of entrance, I have never used them. I've only used the front door and only looked through those others. Thinking now, I must say, I have not once walked behind my home."

She stares blankly, "Oh my, well then, mister lawyer, mister incriminator, you are going to learn your defendant's very art... I'm going to teach you how to break in!"

I roll my eyes at her, "Oh golly."

Already she walks toward the back of the house. Down this path down the side of my home, she turns her head to me, her shoulder following, raising her brow; I reply with a smile, and she laughs. I lengthen my step to catch up to her, and we walk now side by side, her hand grazing mine every few steps just by the swing of her arm.

"I can't believe you haven't walked around your own house!"

"Well, I went in and began to live in it and did all it was that I needed to, nothing more."

"No curiosity?"

"Only necessity."

She means to roll her eyes alone; instead, her whole head turns. We make our way, and with just a push and a kick, we are in. Only seconds inside, she sits down as I grab the basket and extra miscellaneous necessities. I leap upstairs to retrieve a blanket, and in my absence, I hear from below, "A bum bum ba da da da bum bum." The sound of Charlotte pacifying her boredom in song. With every moment near her, my lips never let down a smile. We walk all around my backyard. First, by using my back door just for intrigue, then we take our walk in that misty southern air; the air with that very particular smell, a smell when breathed, ignites instant joy. In our walk, we talk, she sings, and finally, we find, hidden in a secret corner of my vastly luscious green yard, a willow. A willow much larger than those which line my drive, a willow which looks as if to bear the stories of centuries before.

"Aw, poor weeping willow," Charlotte empathizes.

"We should accompany it," I say to see her smile. To which she does.

As far as I could tell and from what she expressed, Charlotte was utterly mystified by our picnic and our talks and laughs, the day in its entirety. In fact, towards its end, she told me, just as I feel, that she finds it hard to remember that we have only just met. From her words and her smile, I am completely positive I am not only a one-sided lover.

Reader, I hope in my words you can understand this, what should be called a situation perhaps. I hope you can see the smile which glazes Charlotte's eyes; I hope you can feel my heart's ache and bare my same gleam. I hope that in these pages, you may understand the preposterous, puerile love I feel towards my little beauty.

16

Day after day, I wake up to myself and the sun to share time with Charlotte, then fall back to bed in the presence of the moon. In these days, Charlotte and I work some, we walk to "our Willow," so she calls it, and so sweet in her "ours" she speaks. We eat by my large table's side, and sometimes she reads in my study, and we laugh, and we talk. But today is the day that has been marked for a near two weeks not only by myself but my dear Charlotte. The day, of course, which all of my things shall be arriving from Maine, all of my things which piece by piece make up my old life, my sad, lonely life which I lived before meeting Charlotte. In these weeks here, I've lived as a monk—a minimalist with no possessions, only bare necessities, which at the beginning of these weeks was an annoyance, but in these last days, I have barely noticed the lack of décor or clothing, or plates or even of drapes. Charlotte is my only need. As I put on my shirt and trousers, I believe I will be throwing out quite a bit.

Today not only do I have the excitement of the arrival of my possessions, but Charlotte is coming even earlier this morning to eat breakfast. Her excitement for today has been nearly peculiar; why should she be so excited to unpack alongside myself? In my expecting her, I stand against the column on my porch in order to view her leap across our small field and watch her gleam. Waiting to hear the creak of her door, I watch the willow's branches sway ever so slightly in the wind. I must say that the willow is my most favorite of trees only because it is more sorrowful than myself and does not take pity on me, for I may take pity on a weeping willow, but its beauty does not allow for such.

At last, her voice rings, "William!" She speaks so delighted, drawing out my name, emphasizing the "Will" in an attempt of British tone. Just as predicted, she leaps, and she gleams, and I am eased with ludicrous happiness. I begin to make my way in, ahead of her, because I know she will rush to my side. I already hear her up those steps. She, so beautiful in the morning, her face so bright, though her eyes still tired, her small waist, and freshly brushed hair. While eating, we, like always in each other's company, talk; we discuss all matters, but today for the first time in depth, she dares to speak of her parents and of her home. How much I learn in but fifteen minutes about life inside those walls; more than I could have ever imagined from looking through the glass. My happy darling just lost her young brother, to which the stun of the event has caused her mother to go mute; she has been paralyzed and has not left her chair since the tragedy. Her father has just returned from somewhere, where she is not even sure may be, but he arrived last night drunk, so it sounds, for when he arrived to find his wife still strapped to that same chair, he could only turn his rage to Charlotte. The rage revealed as she took off her cardigan. I believe this is why she is telling me about her life, to save herself from the questions and from drawing attention to the bruises. My poor angel, my sad doe. My pity does not stay long before transforming into rage. How I wish to strangle this father of hers, how I wish for his neck to turn bluer than my dear's arms. How I wish to shake her mother back to existence, to tell her, her daughter who lives in the flesh must live alone in pain, and grief, feed herself, pay for her way all as you fade away from reality. And most of all, I wish to tell Charlotte how sorry I am for her, that I wish I could take her away from it all, that we could live, her and I, and that I should surround her with nothing but love. Instead, I put my hand on her knee, which she immediately takes with her own. Tears start to swell. As soon as the first drops, she flees from her chair into my arms. My dearest's pain is simply too much for a girl to take. Yet, I sit as the selfish man I am, for in her grief, I have her in my arms. Her tears fall, just as her hair, into my face. I feel her lips graze my neck as she whispers, "I'm sorry." I urge, "No, no. My darling, do not be sorry." She says nothing, but I feel her soft smile. I always saw a sort of sadness in her eyes, but I had never guessed for her life to be so trifling. It did not take long before she was through with her pain, finished drawing attention to her brokenness. She looks instead out the front window, "Oh look there, what marvelous timing!" The trucks, of course, managed to save her from the discussion, which she would have avoided either way. Three trucks it took, and with four men, six counting myself and Charlotte, we quickly unload the boxes and place them in any open space we can find; in the foyer, in the dining room, the great room, anywhere appears fine for these men who just wish to be gone. So, they receive their wish, and Charlotte and I begin to move and unstack some things. As they depart, another car appears to take their place in my drive; I turn to Charlotte, "How popular I am today." She laughs. Anything I can do to make her laugh.

A most haughty appearing man appears, taking his time from his car in his grey suit; he examines the house. Slowly, he turns back to his car for his briefcase. Immediately I know, I can all but sense this man, a parallel acquaintance—a lawyer.

"Hello, Sir." I expel, holding back the slightest bit of cheer.

He replies, "You are William."

"Indeed."

"I am your aunt's lawyer."

What did I say! Only what is so despairing is that I had believed all matters of law concerning my aunt to have been finished and complete in Maine. Apparently, one last account was left unsaid, the matter of her car. How completely mysterious as I had the slightest idea, she had a vehicle which is perhaps why this is the only legal matter left undone. Uncovering the story, my aunt had kept her very late husband's car in a storage garage and had seemingly forgotten about it, and now it is to be mine. This morning, not only have I discovered the intrinsic design of Charlotte's horrid abode and received my belongings, but now I am said to be given a car! Well, I have just been orally delivered a car this morning. The vehicle itself is to arrive at a later date just like my luggage. Although, with the business of the car now settled, I meet Charlotte inside to find her diligently moving boxes. Looking to me with those sad eyes, I know what I need to do; I tell her, "Charlotte, that man has just come to tell me I will be receiving a car."

"Oh gee, that's real swank!"

I laugh, restraining myself, "Yes, yes, and possibly when said car appears, I may take you somewhere, to shop or to a restaurant. Out of this town where you could escape your parents for a day."

With barely any time for thought, "Would you really? William, that sounds wonderful, yes!"

She leaps for my arms once again to hug me in thanks. If just the promise of taking her away should leave her this grateful, what act will her gratefulness bring upon truly being taken away?

"Alright, well, we have some work to do." She draws us back to reality, back to time and she is right, we do have much work ahead.

As you know, I am one man, and as a singular man, I do not have many possessions; at least I did not think so, but I have since received my aunt's furniture and décor. You see, she was very classy, a living definition of elegance, an English woman at heart hidden deep behind her transfixed accent and American spirit. Her home, our home, resembled the finest Georgian style, now quite fitting in title at least. As we unpack the wood, hand-crafted chairs, desk, and bed frame, Charlotte is nothing but amazed. I assure her all of it belonged to my aunt, and I perform quite poor on the matter of interior design. Charlotte though appears to be quite fond of it all, I come to find. Not only do I have my own possessions, mostly complied of books, clothes, and office accessories, I have my aunt's and the previous owner's leftovers, which just so happen to fit in quite nicely among my own things. I don't remember if I have mentioned, but the interior of this house was actually in superior shape upon my arrival; I have since cleaned it, yes, for it was very dusty, and I painted some of the walls, but the molding and overall structure was nearly perfect, far more than I can say for the exterior. So, at the sheer perfectness of the interior and for the saving myself from further labor, I allow myself to spring into unpacking with my Charlotte. Charlotte has already placed most of my furniture in my bedroom and study, although I performed the heavy lifting, she commanded me about to match her own design. We hang some paintings about the rooms, but now we reach the main event, which Charlotte has come for, the shelving of the books. She unpacks, "Dickens... Homer... Aurelius... Austen— wait, Austen? Jane Austen, like Mr. Darcy!" She chants especially emphasizing the British tone. What excitement she finds in gilded leather, which I had not believed another soul may bare. Onto the discovery of the law texts, she describes, "Very large, very thick!" I hear discouragement, although it isn't long until I hear her sing, "How marvelous!" She exclaims in all seriousness. She'd made a space specifically designated for each of the books she wished to read. I offer to allow her to take any book she pleased, but she warns it would be burned or torn, or worse. I couldn't imagine much worse. "Well, then you should just read here," I tell her. She smiles in confirmation of the invitation. As if it had only been moments since that lawyer had come, we remain dazzled by the fact the light had crawled away. Charlotte and I had unloaded, moved, and shelved all day, as in the presence of one another, boredom maintains no existence. Charlotte seems that because of her extended stay, either she should find her parents passed out, if she was lucky, possibly one gone entirely, or enraged, and upon her return, she would be fastened into a horrible place. I hoped she would find them vanished entirely, so she would return to me where she would stay, protected from any gruesomeness of the world, and in peace; she, a goddess, could stay with me, and this house could become her Heaven on Earth. She stands in my doorway, abnormally pale and trembling, so this night, I walk with her beyond the porch onto the grass. No lights appear to be gleaming through the windows, so I follow Charlotte closely. As she goes in, I crouch at the side of her home beneath the window. How funny I feel; if anyone were around to bear witness to such a scene as this, I know I would be shot immediately in the belief I was a criminal, but this I must risk for the safety of my love, for love will make a man do much more than this. Hearing the door shut ever so softly with no noise beyond this sound, not a voice or even a breath, I remain. I wouldn't leave until I had given her enough time to get to her room to change and fall asleep. The idea that such a beautiful, happy soul could be treated so horribly gives me a new appreciation for the life I was able to lead in my youth, although angering me so with how they must suppress her happiness, ignore her triumphs, and bruise her from the outside in. How I wish to bring an end to them.

In my spiral, I seemed to have forgotten where I was for a moment; realizing now, I flee immediately, knowing my Charlotte is, in fact, safe.

17

12:00 pm. To be precise, 12:23 pm, and not a single sight of Charlotte, not an exchange of glance or conversation, no breakfast together, no helping me unpack. She had not made me any promises of coming, but after last night I have every right to worry, to think of the worst, that is all, you see I am simply worried for Charlotte, not to be mistaken by any bit of upset from remaining in her absence.

I have been unloading my kitchen all morning, organizing cutlery and stacking plates. All in complete silence. No talk, no laughter. Weeks ago, I would be at total peace, but now with Charlotte, I am unable to go on, to think clearly without breathing the very air of her breath. My aunt's clock ticks louder; the time, now 12:30 pm. What to do? Where to find Charlotte? I cannot go to her house; her parents can't know I'm the man she gives all her waking hours to, however lucky I am to be that man. Where could I go? At last, a thought! Without hesitation, I fly out the door, and with another outlandish practice just beginning since my time in the South, I do not hesitate to even think to lock my door; there is just no need. How liberating it feels to fly out of my house without a moment overrun by a battle between a key, how motion picture it feels as I fly about my porch's edge. I, though worried, will not run to seek my dearest. If it were to be that she and I were the only two in this town, I may run, but instead, I stroll, yes, I stroll down the gravel road from my home to my kind man's store. I wave at the neighbors out and about, and I even smile at the kind man and his wife, but as soon as I believe my kindness and small talk to be enough to distract from the very question I was about to ask, I find a pause and then, "Stewart, may I ask if you have seen Charlotte in town today?" I ask as nonchalantly as a man so deep in love could.

"Yes, she has been hanging around. But why do you ask? Do you know her well?" he replies guessingly.

"Why yes, she has been helping me unpack my things, specifically the sifting through of my books, and I was just going to give her a book we talked about, one which I have finally found to give to her," I speak only in the most innocent of a voice, telling the story only as it is.

Before he can speak again, I am pulled into an aisle, "What, you are spying on me now! Are you William? Well, you're not doing so well. You just gave us away! You don't ask for me. Stick to working on your house, why don't you?" Charlotte lectures in her most witty voice.

"Charlotte, I'm not spying on you. I had to find you because after the information I received yesterday and taking you home last night, I was worried." I reply with utmost sincerity, though internally I puzzle at what she thought it was I was giving away, her words, "giving us away." Does this mean that to her there is an us?

"I was only kidding; I got it. And I didn't come over because I was here getting us some pop and lunch as a thank you." She says with the reprisal of her typical angelic tone.

"Why Charlotte, I do not expect you to give up all your time to me," immediately before I could move to my next point,

"I know you don't, but I would really love to if you still want me."

"Of course, I would want you, and I cannot believe you would spend your own money on me; please let me pay you back."

Letting out a grunt, "I made the lunch, and the pop was just a few cents, and I'm sure you can make it up to me somehow." She proceeds providing me her nymphetic grin (a wink per se without the gayness).

"I must owe you quite a lot since you are the one doing the work for me."

She glances around for a moment, then speaks, "Well, I think when you get this car of yours, and you keep your promise, you will have well paid me back in full. Now let's get out of this place; the number of tools in here is suffocating."

Her words seem to cause an internal combustion of emotions. Her words which she turns into riddles and poems, flood my mind with ecstasy and wonder. How from your talk you have put us together, your hints at a future, how could I love Charlotte so tragically that I would kill for her, and still, it is not anger I possess, it is the wish for the loosening of her grip which is driving me to this insanity. She speaks mindlessly and innocently, and I sit, counting down the seconds to when I should see her again, jumping to my window anytime I hear the slightest of a noise to seek her; Charlotte, a nymphet whose dress is white, floats through clouds over flames of Hell which reflect in her eyes.

As Charlotte commands, we leave that tool-drenched store and walk to "our" willow by my home on the road which I have just taken, yet this time with no hospitable neighbors or noise to interrupt, only her and I alone. She carries her drink, and I, mine with the food.

"I just love summer!" she spits out.

"As do I. Tell me, what do you love about the season?" I ask her.

"I love... Well, I believe I love the freeness, you know how there's no real responsibility, the longer days that just make you feel like there is never a rush, the activities, the   outfits (she points to her own). But you know what! Well, never mind."

"What is it, Charlotte?" I pull.

"My favorite thing, what I really love about summer, is the air, but listen before you ask why; it has this very particular smell that you never smell in any other season, and it just feels special. It just changes your whole, well, I don't know." she stops.

"I know exactly what it is that you mean."

Really can we be so much of the same? It is the air that possesses me; it is the air that makes summer so wondrous, only I never expected Charlotte to believe much of the same. She, of course, denies my understanding, so I finish her phrase, "The air, it smells of grass after rain, and of never-ending time, it smells of joy and of summer love, and it provokes a new identity in someone. Although now you probably find me silly."

Sincerely she speaks, "No, you understand it too." Before we can walk but three feet more, she announces, "We should start a club, the summer-air smellers! How ridiculous would we sound!" Not yet at our willow, we walk side by side, our shoulders finding one another every other step. Charlotte smiles, "Hey, let's take a shortcut. Come on through here."

Standing back, I ask, "You better not be taking me and my loafers through any mud pits."

"No, I am not taking you or your loafers through any mud pits." She mocks, imitating my voice, especially on the "loafers and "mud-pit." I give in, unsurprisingly, and follow blindly. The shortcut taking us through a field, then by a river, over a small bridge, through a field with an assemblage of trees, and then, "Aha!" She chants. "This is not our willow." She strains. "Darn!" She exclaims again. She continues to walk further into the woods. Still, we both carry our unopened bottles and lunch, then she adds, "Well, this will have to do; we can visit our willow soon." She has us sitting at a lake, completely secluded and completely beautiful. As I unload the food, "We should come swimming here!" she speaks abruptly.

"Aren't there alligators in Georgia?" I question.

"Such a Maine-lander. Alligators are in the southern part of Georgia. We are in the north." she enlightens me.

"Well then, aren't we lucky."

"We are indeed because now you will go swimming with me!" she urges.

In seeing how Charlotte's daily fashion is what you may call nontraditional in comparison to the majority, fashioned with shorter hems (much shorter) and breezy tops forcing the projecting of her bare midriff; I cannot dare to dream of what provocative suit she may wear while swimming. How I would love to admire her skin's glow in the sun once splashed with water.

"Charlotte, I should love to go swimming with you." I give in.

"Oh, wonderful! You know William, you really are swell." she states.

"Why is that?" I wonder.

"You let me read your books, you make sure I'm safe, you promise to take me out and to do my favorite things with me, and I thought you talking to me was enough." How heartfelt she speaks, not in her ordinary voice, but how glad I am for the change. Before she spoke, I never realized such a beauty could be satisfied by my candor alone.

"Darling, you could not fathom how grateful I am for your company," I tell her truthfully.

"We sure were meant to find each other." she replies peacefully, immediately retreating to her sandwich.

"We" and "meant"—the two words she uses to describe this skinny love, the power of her words, fingering Moonlight Sonata on the keys of my soul. We eat in no hurry, and we stay a little while. I watch Charlotte as she attempts to skip rocks on the water, but she decides she is done, and we begin our walk home. Upon arrival, we both appear to feel unfulfilled in our shorter time together. So, she comes inside, picks up a book (a book of legal text, very brave) and reads her page then, asks a question, then reads for a little while longer, then finds a more comprehensive question and a need for a more in-depth answer so she may walk from her place on the couch to me at my desk, throwing her arms in a loop around me holding the book over my head, she places the text down onto my desk, relieving the book from her grip, then resting her arms down upon my shoulders, leaning her head around mine. She seems to have asked something on the matter of incrimination, but I do not remember specifically because you will find, this next moment blocks all noise, for as I turn my head to look my questioner in the eyes, she peers down, raising her brow, and parting her lips. All I can do is stare inwardly into her eyes and then down to her lips, completely frozen as she moves inward; I feel the humiliating adjustment of my lips which she proves unnecessary, as I feel hers on my ear, "So, mister lawyer, what's the answer?" Allowing her mouth to linger as she moves to her previous position. My precocious tease. I am forced to give her a completely ridiculous answer, but as long as it sounds compelling and eloquent, she has always believed me. Charlotte, you see, she pushes any boundaries there may be further each day when it has only just been a matter of weeks. The moon saves me, moving in on my lust and shining so bright for Charlotte to notice it is time to leave and to leave me to my deepest desires which play out in her absence when the night is completely dark and finds it time to leave me to my own darkness.

18

A new day. My dearest darling awaits. 9:30 am. She knows by now that I have done all of my morning duties, so she sits on my porch awaiting my presence. I join her on that brand new build, and in the morning serenity, we awake to the world. Over the course of my reawakening here in Georgia, I ordered a refrigerator, one which came in the mix of unboxing all other belongings. Thankfully with the incentive of extra cash, the men even installed the thing, but the issue I face today is that I have nothing to fill the large box with; therefore, Charlotte has made it her duty to devise a list and a date to retrieve said list, hence, today. Fully awake, we set off from our seats on the porch and walk down my drive, willows weeping as we pass. Charlotte had once informed me she was quite spiteful of the man who runs the main store; you remember, the most awkward man, bald, equipped with glasses and uniformed. She informs me today of each and every neighbor we pass, every terrible marriage, each happily sickening young love, of the illiterate teacher, the creep, and of the few rarities. The rarities being the kind, considerate, non-annoyingly hospitable type, such as Stewart, who we find ourselves off to visit today. I can't help but believe Charlotte's descriptions of our neighbors are simply humorous predictions, but she assures all is true and that she knows it to be true because she has lived in this grueling town for all of her life, and in that life, she has fixated herself on learning the difficulties of others to relieve herself of her own. How can I not believe her words after such a testimony?

As we step into the store, her list follows, escaping from her pocket. Basket in hand, she launches. Milk, jam, eggs, cheese, strawberries, blueberries, pop, and a watermelon. All items, quite unarguable. As I check out and make some conversation with Stewart, I notice Charlotte has been waved away by her repugnant friends. In the corner of my eye, I bear witness to the scene; them huddling and snickering; though they (her friends) look ridiculous, Charlotte does not take part in such a juvenile regrouping. When she laughs, she does not have braces that withhold her mouth from opening beyond a certain extent; her skin glows as the moon when her friends are nothing but the resemblance of craters on its surface. She does not stand with an awkward shift and turn, but she stands deep holding her ground. To any sound man of my prime who may overlook this group, he may see no difference in Charlotte in beauty or charm, just a group of girls. Only the genius (or the insane) can recognize the dominance she holds at the clasp of her hands or the grace she sheds at the turn of her knee to step away.

"William, are you done?" she asks.

"Oh yes... Just finished." I respond, making my way to her.

"This is Madeline and Jane." she introduces.

"Hello, Madeline. Jane." I greet.

"William got a new refrigerator, so we are shopping for it. We shouldn't let these groceries get too warm before they can see their new home. So... bye, guys." she dismisses.

"Goodbye Madeline, Jane. Until next time—" all I can get out before being pushed out by Charlotte.

"They are such airheads; talking to them is humiliating." she explains.

This catches me off guard. In her behavior just now, I witnessed some differences between her from the group, but I would not have guessed it was all a ruse.

"Why is that now?" I question honestly.

"Well, they can't talk about anything other than boys in our classes and whether Mrs. Langford is having an affair or not. Oh, I'm sorry, I nearly forgot; there is also the occasional chatter of 'should I roll my godly length skirt up a notch so that I may show my whole ankle?' They have no substance, no motivation." she explains as though this is a subject in which she has dissected at length.

"Now, Charlotte, I am sure they are fine girls; they are just still immature and—" I try to ease her, but she interrupts,

"Yeah, immature, and the sad thing is, they are the only two near my age worth even talking to. Not even just near my age, practically anyone else as well. No one here cares about literature or politics or science, or philosophy. They have no care for anything. I don't even know how they live!"

All she explains must be why she seems so fond of me; I am the complete composure of all that she has mentioned just now. How in her eyes, I must illuminate perfection.

"Charlotte, I know this town seems inescapable now, but you have years and years to live—" Again, in my wholehearted attempt of a response, she interrupts,

"Well, until then, I will spend my time with you, the little piece of the world I long for."

How those words should flutter through my ears for the rest of the day. As the dramatics die down, Charlotte and I could walk straight again until once more, we are stopped,

"William?" an only slightly familiar voice searches.

"Come on!" Charlotte demands.

"Keep on walking Charlotte, and I will run if I have to in order to catch up to you." I soothe her.

"You better." she exalts.

The man from which the voice directs immediately introduces himself; he, being Charlotte's teacher. Nearly forty, it seems, almost of my height, a tad bigger than me in mass, and very southern. He verbally runs from my introduction to his interrogation. Phrases such as, 'I hear Charlotte is helping you,' 'fine girl she is,' and the real heavy hitter, 'You two seem to be spending a great deal of time together.' I knew immediately in his voice, and now in his questions that he too is a devilish admirer, who now faces jealousy. But with school being out, with Charlotte in my presence, and walking my halls, I do not feel threatened. Charlotte did not even say hello to him! He is a distant admirer, that is all, and so in a few minutes more of friendly conversation, I dismiss him and all because, well, 'Charlotte is waiting,' of course. How I am sure, his heart is torn. But I have not a moment to care for the man for my Charlotte is indeed waiting.

I reach the top of the hill, and below I see her walking just as I had told her to, and so just as I also told her, I run to meet her. Is this a run, or only more of a speedier gait? Quite possibly just a change in gait, but an Englishman does not run. Although, what must I say, Charlotte has my ways of life deteriorated. In our rejoining, she finds the company of her smile again, and to my astonishment, she does not but mention the name of her teacher or even ask what it was he would have had to say. Does she even know this man? Regardless we reach home, and with the cold items still in hand. Charlotte neatly places each item on its very own shelf, creating a museum for herself in a mockery of how little I have even after a grocery run. As she tries to take all the food from a singular cabinet and place each item in a cabinet of its own, I catch her, leading her to retreat to my study. She has me know that she finds it strange for so few possessions to be in one large house; lonely she calls it, but she also has me know she finds it regal in a way. I had not thought of it before her explanation, that being with so little, there is nothing on the tops of the tables or counters or barely the walls, only a few statement pieces like a palace.

"Oh, a palace, how I wish I could have been born a royal," she comments, "William, you could see me as a Duchess or Baroness, couldn't you?" she asks.

"I could see you as the most esteemed and beautiful of royalty. Why not a Princess?" I tease.

"I could be anything in your eyes; how fantastic! I wouldn't want to be a Princess or even a queen because they are simply much too overrated. You know the whole, 'save me, Prince Charming, save me,' and the cliches concerning the queen. A Duchess or Baroness just sound much more scandalous, so eloquent."

How feminist Charlotte can be at times. Her character is one that is so hard to pin, changing at any moment, yet always somehow smooth with never an action out of place. I believe this is what makes her Charlotte. What makes her my love. This whole conversation which was sparked by Charlotte's refrigerator stocking seemed to have led Charlotte to the idea that we should walk to our willow and read there today. I, with no counter plan, agree. And so, we head to our willow until the sun and the moon should swap places. The summer air evokes a certain emotion most prevalent in the night, reminding me of how in that summer day, I may have spent all hours with only my love to dance and play. How I would in days long gone, days before Charlotte, not have even breathed a breath of air from that summer day. How in the night, secrets will spill, and the sound of deep conversation will overcast the chirp of the crickets. The night, where the only light is from the moon, feels safer than any moment in the day. And the moonlight shines, and the willow's branches sway in the soft wind, illuminated only slightly for their sage glows to waver about the night sky. A path for Charlotte's walk home, illuminated along with the leaves. She grabs my hand to lift it and let it loose as her goodbye, her soft touch just shaking my hand. How I feel her walls caving, her heart opening; what more I may feel is in store.

"Goodnight, William." she sings with the stars reflecting in her eyes.

"Goodnight— my Charlotte."

19

Sunday. I awake to the sounds of the birds. Feeling proactive and too early to see Charlotte, I decide I should check in on my car's delivery date if I could, which means venturing out onto Main Street. Getting myself to leave as early as possible, I'm on the road. Now, with only seventeen minutes passed since setting off out of bed, I find not but one prostitute-resembling woman or hillbilly man to stop me on my journey. Making my way into the store to use the phone, I find there is no Stewart either. In fact, his store is not even open. Not that feverish man, nor is his door open. The makeshift post office— locked as well. What apocalypse must have presented itself to the town in the night? I stand dumbfounded, wandering in search of life. Changing my path to walk home, I can hear music, yes— an organ, and voices, down a small gravel route, meant only for foot traffic. I follow the noise to a hidden white farmhouse appearing structure, and without hesitation, I open one of its large doors, immediately hearing only the echo of its deafening groan. The music stops, and as my eyes fix to find the first face I may meet, I see Charlotte up left-center stage wearing her lilac dress. Though as two little boys' laughter fills the air, they draw my attention to every other face surrounding me, which just so happens to be that of every other face in the town. And with the interruption of the lady's gasps, my eyes move to the large cross situated behind Charlotte, who stands only smiling at me, the only one on the premises who still may wish to look at me with an ounce of joy, regardless my view of the cross, and the mere fact that today is Sunday, I realize moments much too late that what meeting I have just rudely stumbled upon is what happens to be the gathering of worship of the Lord, in other words, Sunday church service. How may I ever receive a pass to Heaven now? All I can think to do is sit. An usher takes the door from me, and miraculously as he closes it, there is neither a groan nor an echo. I sit, turning to find a woman to my right who looks to be a living corpse, with hair as pale as her complexion, and a darkest of dress as if she were planning on attending her own funeral. I saw Charlotte was trying to keep in her laughs as she witnessed the whole fiasco front and center. To my thankfulness, the preacher said not a word of my entrance. He must not be one to work the unexpected into a sermon. I could only imagine... "A man! Church, a man has appeared to us! You may see this man as an interruption, but I tell you, this man's coming is going to be just like the second coming of the Lord! Amen church! Out of nowhere. Loud. No, roaring! And quick!" I could only thank God this pastor was not one for improv, and that no more attention was drawn to my arrival.

Without further hesitation, the noise begins again, and I come to learn; Charlotte is also an angel of music; her voice louder than all of the others, so vivid. A voice that can be heard over the instruments even. As she sings her glories to the Lord, her smile never ceases. She had never shared with me her devout nature nor asked of mine. For your information, I have no particular religious interest, and so sitting through hours of a church service has not been an activity that I have done, nor do I find myself in enjoyment of. Though, for Charlotte, I made the sermon into more of a history lesson. One titled "The Roman Empire versus Christ," and the songs are already completely bearable as mine truly is the one to sing them.

After the service, this is where Hell begins; every occupant of the town gathered in one building. As soon as the preacher prays and wishes us all a good day each person flogs to my seat for introductions, questions, statements, cards, anything and everything to bring the attention to me, but out of all the people, not a single face is Charlotte's. Over the mob, I look to every corner, every staircase, out every window; I watch the door, and still no Charlotte. My heart aches at the loss of her sight, therefore my mission becomes to retreat as fast as possible. I tell the crowd I must be getting home for 'an important shipment coming in,' this is a lie, so another stone shall be cast onto me for sinning in a church, but what is new. After the series of 'Please come next Sunday,' the 'Aws,' the goodbyes, and the 'Just let us know if you ever need anything, really anything at all,' my perfect performance hiding any insults, sarcastic remarks, and eye rolls comes to an end, and I leave that church a seemingly kind and swell man. Finally, air that hasn't been circulated by the breath of ninety-five hicks. But before I can step out of the door frame, I am startled by an abrupt voice, come to find it is Charlotte.

"You came to church today. How swell! Finally, a face out there I want to look at. Oh, did you like my singing?" she frantically ponders.

My heart that ached upon losing her, rejoiced in the knowing she had been waiting for me all the while. We walk to town together, and she persuades me to get her some candy before going home. Forcing me by saying it was the least I could do to pay her back for interrupting her song, reminding me church starts at 10:00 am on the dot. As we walk, I tell her how beautiful she sang, and she tells me, in exchange, every detail of how her holy life came to be. Come to find out, she began attending church as a way to escape her home, then she was roped into singing in the choir. She actually despises being there; she says the ladies always scold her for her skirts being too short, and the pastor questions her lifestyle too fervently for her liking. Ultimately, she has me to escape to now, which means she does not need the church. Although, I tell her I would begin to come and she could sing for me, so she smiles and only asks if I would torment her for her skirt hem, to which I most undoubtedly explain to her that her bare skin is angelic and should be out for God to see. She laughs, I too with her, and there she shows me that nymphetic grin which holds one hundred words, which today I read as she did not only see my line as a mere joke but that she has uncovered my real means, my lust for her bare skin, lust she could look in the eye and fondle with just the placement of her smile. In these instances, it becomes difficult to push aside my erotic urges, to hide them far below my skin, but she only makes for further difficulty as she skips away, with each hop flinging her skirt up into the air. Her face holds only a smile which she sheds back to me every three hops or so to see if I have melted away in complete libido. She holds her bag of candy in her hand, which she leaves untouched until our walk is made complete. She comes with me to my home to further expand her escape. I follow her as she sits on the porch, one leg on the step, one hanging, while her skirt falls in between. Continuing the subject of divinity, Charlotte states, "You know I go to church for the word; it is the people that ruin it. But I do love God and trust and all. And I pray, and I know I'm going to Heaven, and I can't wait for that day because I will finally be rid of my horrible father. And my mom can see her son again, and I can just be at peace." I have not but an idea of how to reply to her. I am not a Christian, but in order to be with her for all eternity, I vow to her before the Lord, "Charlotte, I shall be in that church every Sunday until my death. I know abrupt, but today is the day I change." And to my astonishment, Charlotte does not speak; instead, she comes to my side and simply sits, laying her head on my shoulder. Taking her hand in mine, laying our hands intertwined on my leg, she whispers, "This is peace." Her being so close to me, I can feel as though she can hear my heartbeat; I try so hard to control its pace, but it soars in her embrace; transcendent rapture has come. Before I could allow seconds for my overcome self to rationalize, to think at all before I may even blink again, I reach my chin up slightly to place my lips to her forehead, holding them there for only a mere two seconds. In their release, Charlotte moves closer, and I let my head rest upon hers. And on this Sunday morning, with the willow as my witness, my soul has been fully delivered, branded in steel with my Charlotte's signature forever engraved on my heart.

As the willow's branches sway in that southern air, Charlotte and I sit, both in peace. Her head lays on mine, unmoving for nearly half an hour. This time as we sat, only looking off onto a faraway place, one of us would blurt out at random some philosophical thought. That is until a huge surge of rain came from the sky completely out of the blue, our heads covered by the porch, but our legs utterly drenched. The sun, peeking through, with only a few clouds limiting its brightness, mist already forming from the touch of the rain on the heated ground. At first, Charlotte launched back below shelter, but her white skirt was already drenched and my light trousers with them. It only took her a moment to analyze the situation, until leaping out of cover onto the grass, throwing her shoes onto the porch past my side. She gleams, "Come on William, what is better than the summer rain!"

I take a bit longer of an analysis for the consideration of the absurdity of the situation, and the carelessness of Charlotte, disregarding her drenched white cloth, her natural form peering through. Without the means to my own mind, shall I agree to partake in Charlotte's lunacy? Throughout my entire examination, Charlotte dances and twirls, grabbing the hem of her skirt, pulling with both hands from side to side. Her laugh never at rest, "Ok!" Taking off my shoes, although still under the porch. Charlotte cheers when she catches sight of both shoes undone. Before stepping foot off my security, she pulls me down into the storm; taking my hand, we run around my house. We continue to run, spinning across the field. She leaps higher than ever, so it seems. Abruptly, she stops, turning to me, then to our tree, then back to me as if to draw more attention to the location. Charlotte stands in her blouse of lace and her smocked skirt, while I stand in amazement at her, dressed in my white button-up and cream trousers, us both in supreme indecency.

"Dance with me, William!" she rejoices in a British tone,

"Charlotte, I don't dance."

"That's what all men say, and yet all men can!" Immediately, she pulls me near to her after such an exclamation.

I do indeed dance; I was quite the debutante, so she is right. Throwing her arms to my shoulders and mine gracefully to her waist, her bare, thin waist; the feeling of my hands on her soft skin which lines only her rib cage. We waltz shoeless and see-through in the midst of the muddy grass to the music of the world with the rain as the chorus and the thunder for the bridge. She laughs nearly every sway and performs as though she had not a dance in her life; nonetheless, her incessant grace reigns. The entire world vanished in a moment, her and I the only life form, and the sun, our spotlight. Two hopelessly devoted souls staring everlastingly far beyond each other's eyes as we balter in the rain, unconscious of the time as it flies by.

Leaving enough minutes of the hours for the rain to pass us by, Charlotte, not leaving the tree's side. I cannot blame her as I do not wish to leave hers. With all we may do in the moment, we sit down at our tree's side, I, with my back to its bark, and her, with her head in my lap looking into the sun's brightening rays, calling out the shapes she finds in the clouds as they pass, us both taking in the petrichor. The smell that adds to the summer serenity, and maybe in this perfect scene, another hour has passed as we have come witness to the sky's change of color and loss of the sun. With devouring hopes Charlotte would somehow stay with me, she must go. We walk less flavorfully across my field only to part ways at the reach of my back porch, and just as each of the days before, I watch her silhouette fade into the setting sun, with rays of orange and blue beaming by her side. At the loss of her sight, I walk around my house and to the front steps, where I am reminded of my love again— her shoes. How could she have forgotten? I cannot but show up at her door, so they must stay in my shelter. Reaching down to recover the shoe belonging to her left foot, I find her bag of candy spoiled in the water. All of her belongings I bring inside, where we shall all await her return.

The night fell, and with the night came dreams upon dreams of Charlotte and I living out eternity with one another. My nights since our meeting have not been so cruel; the insomnia I once experienced, now long gone.

20

Since our most perfect day together, a day I would have thought unimaginable, a day which could only subside in my dreams, played out unparalleled on that rainy Sunday. A day now long gone, three days past. In those days, Charlotte would stay and help some with the porch or another series of monotonous tasks which would one day add up to make my home the ideal abode.

Today excitement may relish once more, the car will be rolling in and Charlotte is beyond ecstatic. She has already planned our little trip, which will only last a day. It is to take place on a Saturday, for every Saturday, her dad leaves to go to an undisclosed location and does not return until between two to four in the morning; a ritual he has had in place for the last five months, being one in which we can rely on continuing. Charlotte did in fact inform her mother of our plans, and of course, her mom did not agree or disagree. In conversation throughout our time together, I have learned Charlotte has never once ventured into any "big city." Her dream has long been to see New Orleans, but in the time given for this trip, we both know it cannot be done.

The morning had flown by in anticipation, and noon had settled in its place. Charlotte and I walk to Main Street, where the man and the car shall meet us. We walk, paying extra attention to the gravel in the grass, waving to every neighbor on our way, and smiling at every child on a bike who passes us by because we know in only a moment, we should not have the need to make this walk anymore. Our feet should not hit the gravel; our waves would only be too slow for the speed of the car. We know we should walk this route again, but imagining there is not a need to do so is simply thrilling to our anticipating minds. Savoring each step along our path, we reach our destination— Main Street— full of unfavorable people and scarce machinery, making it all the more easier to find the car. In front of the barbershop, she sits with her driver, a black 1938 Lincoln K-Series V12 Touring Coupe. How could my aunt come to own and never use such a beauty? That is, it was an inheritance from her late and most wealthy husband, who taught me how to drive when I first arrived in Maine, but in only my first year with them, he departed. She did not wish to see his prized possession in the hands of any other, thereby preserving it untouched. I do promise her that the car shall live on as a reminder of the fine man he was, and it shall possess the joys of all of our memories, though concise, considerably fond.

The key-bearing man's enthusiasm is far from near a level to match that of mine and Charlotte's. He stands just ten feet away, leaning onto the car, smoking, and twisting the keys around his fingers. We approach, "Hello, Sir. I am William Hathaway, the recipient of this car." Not a word, just a puff of smoke and a hand gesture to signify the need to see a form of identification. I am luckily well aware of the language of car-folk. As soon as I can manage to show him the papers he so wishes to see, he begins at last to speak, informing us on any extra details, specific quirks he noticed on the drive, and of course, to complete, a spiel formulated by his car delivering company whose name was not even revealed. Upon giving him directions to the shop where he should wait until his ride to Maine or wherever he intends to travel, arrives, he leaves us. With that, Charlotte whips the keys from my hands, immediately unlocking her side of the car, getting in to admire its leather bench seat, sliding to my side to roll down the window. Finally, upon my wait, she tosses me the key. I may get into the car now, unaware of how the car could truly manage to retrieve so many memories— from my first time in it to my uncle. I only pray the car's wheel beneath my fingers may automatically allow my body to remember how to drive. I sit there, holding the wheel, examining the car, nearly pressing its petals, checking its mirrors, that is, until Charlotte chimes in, "So, you gonna drive or what?"

"Yes, Yes. I am getting to that." I reply hastily.

"And I am getting impatient." she informs.

I wait so long in order to worry efficiently, but for the satisfaction of Charlotte, I begin the car. I shift the automobile into motion, and so, we begin. With Charlotte in glee, I confess to her I have not driven in years and that she should not laugh at my capabilities (whatever they may be). Though, as expected, she breaks such an agreement immediately upon affirming my wish. We begin to roll down the hill, and for the first moment, Charlotte only laughs. Her laughs cease as we begin heavily accelerating down said hill; she yells, "Well, don't just steer! Brake or shift or something!" I do, and the doom machine dies down. Upon knowing of our safety's return, she waits not but a moment to laugh once again; now, I with her. Thankfully my home is a straight path from here on; the only turn I face is that of the one into my drive. We drift forward down that country road. Meters ahead of my drive, I begin to slow our pace, turning inch by inch into my drive; nearing the house, we grow slower and slower. Charlotte informs me she could walk faster, but she does not dare to leave the machine; she has all the time in the world and knows I am well aware of that fact. Turning the car one last time into position at its perfectly suited space provided by the drive's large end.

"Oh, good heavens." I exhale.

"Yeah, I don't think I want to drive anytime soon; looks stressful." she states.

"Oh no, it is quite the breeze once you get the hang of it." I play it off.

"So, when do you think you will get the hang of it?" she questions just before adding, "It better be before we go to Athens!"

At last, the location of which she so yearns to go, Athens.

"So, you have decided then. A marvelous choice and I do wish to take you to New Orleans as well someday, but Athens will be quite the consolation." I tell her.

"I can't wait; it will be spectacular! I can read on the way. Oh, and we can go all over the downtown, can't we?" she excites.

"Charlotte, we can do whatever you please," I inform.

"Except New Orleans..." she draws.

"Whatever in Athens," I explain, knowing she meant this sarcastically anyways.

Reaching for the handle to exit the car, I wait in the realization that Charlotte still sits admiring the car's every interior detail, grazing the dash and the leather with her hand, eyeing the panel doors, and checking each mirror. What a sight it is, her eyes reflected back to me in the car's mirrors. I move my hand as if I, too, only meant to admire the car. So glad I am to have followed suit, for in just the next minute of analyzing and admiring, she lays herself across the benched seat, laying her neck across my leg and her head in between. I lean upon her to look her in the eyes; in catching mine, she looks to me as though I were her most valuable sight.

"I like this bench seat." She teases.

I tell her I, too, quite enjoy the bench model of seat. I reach my hand upon her head. And in this moment, a moment since that of when I first saw Charlotte, an urge has been silenced- the longing to brush her hair with my fingers as her comb, pushed away, fulfilled. Her hair which lays across my leg and down its side, with pieces grazing upon my hands, my time had come to live out one of my many desires. I sense her as she falls back in release. Her eyes, they draw backward, her blink slows, her breath released with the parting of her lips; she closes her eyes. We both remain in the car, at peace, in a world away we stay for much longer than anyone else could imagine to reside.

21

My days with Charlotte are becoming more complete, reaching a new level of togetherness. A friendship? No, far beyond. Romantic? No, not in an obscene way. Is it some skinny love? Indeed, it is. A Shakespearean play? Maybe. Or A play of our own, two souls consumingly yet secretly in love held hostage by the grip of conventionalism. A man and a girl, a girl and a man. A play to our love would be one no one would dare to see. Maybe an opera, a tragic tale of my love and me, "Charlotte, ma raison d'etre." My days, the best I've had. My nights, streams of desire and lust, which both die under the moon. Another morning, only hours, and my love will come seek me. We have drafted plans for our trip. We, I say, but I mean Charlotte, for I only agree. She has marked on maps and researched using newspapers and magazines to create an itinerary complete even with time between stops, embellished with her addition of secondary alternatives just in case anything may dare to deter her most perfect day. These maps, timetables, lists, and charts scatter from my kitchen table to my desk, to the Chesterfield, and even lie upon the shelves; a little maze she has cultivated, and within the labyrinth lies the piece of perfection. You see, in my time without Charlotte, I clean and dust constantly, organize my bedroom, which always clutters too soon, so it seems. Majorly I read my cases, keep up with the law and the news, of course, to keep me in tune with reality to make sure that when the summer should end, I will still be able to work as a proper lawyer, which my resume has this town to believe I am to be. It seems the time without the company of Charlotte is inescapable, but if Charlotte never left my side, I'm afraid any normal function of living would not be completed.

This particular morning, I organize the mess she has created; stacking the papers into piles according to what type of document they are and what service they perform, placing books back into their position, and cleaning whatever crumbs lay in hiding. My study—now back to its immaculate shape. With the opening of my front door, "Gosh, for someone who doesn't even stick around sober long enough to remember I'm his daughter, he still thinks he has the right to ask me where I am going! Ridiculous!" Charlotte rampages through the door, explaining, "First of all, he is still sleeping, and it is nearly eleven, then he hears me leaving, and all of a sudden, I hear, 'Oh, where do you think you are going?' Well, I tell him I am helping the neighbor again like I have told you; then he goes and makes me feel guilty with his, 'you are always leaving your poor mom to just sit here by herself all day to go out and about helping who knows who.' I tell him, well, I clean, and I even leave her food just in case, and I change her and everything! I mean, come on, he is the one that leaves to go drink and gamble and do whatever else. He is the "dad," the "husband," how can he spend as many hours as he does drinking? He should be dead anyway by now! If only (She speaks under her breath). Whatever. He let me go." I calm her, telling her to come to me. She sits, and I explain how she is entirely correct, how she does all that she can, more than she should, much more, and that she should not be expected to sit and watch over her mom all hours of the day on top of all else. That it is his fault, he does not have to leave, and that she should not have to listen to his remarks. Frankly, if I could, I would kill him myself. Strangle him with my very hands; this I, of course, did not tell Charlotte. She nearly begins to cry; feeling the urge, she sinks her head into my shoulder, suffocating her tears with my skin, biting her lips so hard to not let any noise escape, nearly grabbing some of my own while doing so. My poor dearest Charlotte. If only the world was just her and I. I hold her to let her know her cries are safe with me, but still, she chooses not to inflict them on me. We sit in my study while she attempts to expel the pain while only forcing it in more. She reaches a point where she no longer needs to dry her tears, for there are none. Still, she leaves her head on my shoulder as she works herself back to her charismatic character. Reaching this point, with the maps and papers sprawled about, "So, this Saturday..." she insights.

"If you still wish, we shall go," I tell her.

"I more than wish!" she informs.

This Saturday, she speaks of, only three days away. Seeing the cycle of her rage and tears had run through, she has come to a deceitful conclusion as she informs me that she would not come to my home for the next two days to keep her father away from any delusions. I agree because I, too, believe she should keep him far away from us. I cannot allow him to corrupt our relationship. I even offer to take her to the market to get food for his favorite meal; she can cook for him, I tell her. This idea she loves. Although quite idealistic of me, it was not hard to imagine what a traditional man stuck in the Stone Age would expect from a woman. Charlotte informs me that her mom always used to make him an egg sandwich so appealing to him that it was as if he may make love to the thing itself if only it was a possibility. I believe one should have to look no further into what type of a man her father is by his choice of such a "delicacy" alone. An egg sandwich? An egg sandwich being a favorite of one's food should lead one to the mental hospital alone. Regardless, before our departure, we take some more time to evaluate our plans, review our schedule, and each stop. Matters appear to be far more than settled, upon perfection, if you may; without any mistakes to fix, we shall depart to Main Street.

Despite assuming all necessities for this man's nauseating delicacy, we stay and wander about the store and the town; we walk as slow as the snails at our feet because, in our return, Charlotte must leave. A leave that should last two full days, the longest I have been without her since our meeting, but she has given me an influx of tasks to complete, which I would carry out in her absence, for when she would return and when we will be reunited, we will be on our way to Athens. Take extra attention to the "our," emphasize the 'o' when you pronounce, stretch the 'r' at the word's end, "our;" a word that brings me to delight— "our" trip. The word meaning just her, and I. Charlotte says any level of ecstasy could not match that of her own, but if only she could pull back the skin across my mind or connect mine to hers for her to hear all that lies inside. As much as I may wish for her to be happier than I, it is only and will always be a fantasy alone.

My heart sinks as I witness her waltz across the lawn between her home and my own; as she turns her head to shine her eyes my way one last time, I know I will not see those eyes for a near fifty-two hours. She has indeed, though, given me quite the list. Much for the car and other road trip necessities; for her, these necessities consist of books, a journal, and food, which I thankfully already have in my possession, but I cannot take my dear on a road trip without the proper necessities. I have made plans to go to town once again to obtain some crisps, candies, gum, sodas, and anything else that may catch my eye. How happy I know she should be at the sight of such glorious necessities, the monuments of road trip culture. And happiness is what she needs. So, if I can give it to her, I should in everyway possible. It has always been bizarre to me that Charlotte has not once traveled further than forty-five minutes from this forsaken town. Never a boat ride nor a train, nothing at all. I understand finances were or are lacking and what opportunity may she have had anyhow, but I guess due to my own parent's most selfish travels, I have grown accustomed to the practice. My mother was a nurse in the first World War, and the depression had no toll on her and her painstakingly wealthy husband, so they traveled. Selfishness—they exuded to their young son and to the world, to all the souls lost just previously and those still in turmoil. I—shipped off as a result to my aunt, who, although old and wrinkled lived a life free and kind-spirited; she taught me all I knew as a young boy. She was a mother in my eyes, more than one, I would say probably because I do not know how a mother would behave or love, but from the love I felt for my mom, the love for my aunt compares astronomically. Maybe this is why I wish so badly to take Charlotte away from her life here because it is what my parents did to me in my youth.

I think the reader may think they know otherwise, but perhaps there is a reason for me to give you another analysis. No, perhaps not, for I know before I continue to carry myself miles away in thought, I should bring myself back to my to-do List. The rest of the day without Charlotte, I should pack the books she has asked for, collect the journals, and do what I may with what I find in my home since I have, as you know, already made a trip to Main Street, using any ounce of kindness and/or stagecraft left in me for the day. Her list of books for me: a series of law texts, some psychology, one of Plato's works, and Volume I of *The History of the Decline and Fall of the Roman Empire* (how inquisitive). Why she wishes to have so many large texts for only hours of a ride is far beyond me, but I do hope she reads to me, for when she does, the heavens open. How in only hours apart, still my only thoughts are of Charlotte. To bed, I climb, aware that she should possess my dreams for her laugh does not stop in the day but only grows by night.

22

I slept very late today. It is 10:07 am, an extra three hours of sleep. On a typical day, Charlotte would be making her way up my porch steps, but today there are no feet climbing my steps, maybe this is why I could allow myself to stay in the dark for fewer hours in the day to bear the loneliness which takes Charlotte's place. Today my list finds itself full of mechanic expeditions. The town's auto-man, though used to trucks, should today work on the grandest piece of machinery he may be able to wrench in his lifetime if I should guess. This task should keep me away nearly all day, thereby occupying my mind. Getting dressed, I put on my "work" clothes to assimilate to my expected environment. Coming to the door, I grab a book and a banana for my potential wait.

The shop, further than Main Street— down a backward road, miles and miles, until you meet a small house with a garage by its side and four times the size, halfway filled with cars, the other, open space, and another slot for tools galore. The man to my aid, who goes by the name of Rick, stands in oil-stained overalls with a patch on his chest to the right that holds his name embordered atop it. This sight, funny to me in the sense that there does not seem to be any other employee, yet he must include his name atop the logo of his own business, which already includes it, though I may not laugh at a man's professionalism nor his work. I know I could not do it. So, facing Rick, we talk, as he remains most interested in the car more than payment even. I seem to have come to admire this man; one of taste and uproot interest in his profession. Already, he has gotten to work, though before he briefly led me to this tiny room where I remain with a window looking into the shop and a bench, where it appears I should sit for all the time it should take him.

Three hours and forty-five minutes, and Rick is done. The time of day— 3:03 pm. So, what should one do with their time in the rainy day, I shall drive home, fix myself a meal, clean my study, and dust every other lifeless room, I read, then sleep; a perfect plan. There, I am off after paying Rick, a hefty price indeed, and my drive may begin. Putting the windows down with such ease, I am not short only five hours having been gone. I take a longer route, circling the fields, riding by the houses of brown and grey over a bridge overlooking the water until I should ride and find Main Street again. I come to my first stop sign, "Sir, hello, sir!" I hear a wimpish man cry out, "In the car, you!" He cries again. I look to every other car around to see who the buffoon is talking to, but there is not a single car around; the buffoon is talking to me. I pull slightly further to the side of the road, "Hi, are you Mr. William Hathaway?" he asks, out of breath.

"Indeed, that is me," I tell him.

"Oh, wonderful. I work for the court; I am the acting paralegal, secretary, bookkeeper... stand-in of sorts." I nod in return. "Yes, so we will be working together, and I just haven't been able to track you down. I talked to Stewart, who says you are a fine guy and that you have the car." He adds with a hand emphasizing motion on the 'the' in 'the car.'

"It appears I do have 'the' car. Sir, nice to meet you, and your name?" I ask patiently.

"I am Hubert. Call me Hugh." A ridiculous name, I should only call him Hugh, ever. I reach out to shake his hand, a first impression to leave him in awe of his new counterpart. Hugh is a quite laughable character—fat in face, large in stomach which he utilizes the hiking of his pants and an overly-sinched belt to try to hide, button-down, tightly tucked, hair slicked back but receding on its own, and glaring glasses. Though, I must say, he aims for a professional appeal which I shall honor diligently. He seems to be a fine partner.

"You have an incredible court record, worked at a big firm too, must have been wonderful handling Bouffard versus Dill!" he cuts in. He is obviously well caught up on my preexistence.

"It was. Hugh, I look very much forward to our working together."

His face in astoundment and glee, "I too, Mr. Hathaway. I too!" holding in his excitement.

And here, in this last phrase, I now know why this man is far more appealing than the others; he has barely a trace of an accent. That is it! Not a southern accent, just a naive and hardworking, determined man. Charlotte, too had not adopted much of a southern accent somehow, but her parents are from the North. And Stewart, although with an accent, has the deepest, most rapturous, harsh of southern tone, soothing like nothing of anything I have heard. It must be that the accent is the root of these people's ridiculousness. Hugh has since made his way off, and still, I remain within the only car on the road; swerving back into my place, I continue down, windows still in their downward position and the southern summer air, still blowing, hitting my face. I realize as I drive, my face holds a particular sensation, not from the wind or from squinting to shield my eyes from the sun, but tense in the cheeks; I have a smile on my face, not with Charlotte and not in any abundant joy yet I have a smiling face. Me and my gleam return home, arriving on my porch; when reaching my steps, I face, only for a moment, Charlotte's home. It was only on this porch weeks ago that we first met, where Heaven's doors opened, where my life was brought to a renewal; only thirty hours until she will return again, thirty hours.

23

Last night, I wavered off to sleep in my study while reading until I awoke in the early morning, around 2:00 am, and went to my proper bed, where I stayed asleep until this moment. Late, just as yesterday, to avoid the sun that would shine on my skin alone. 10:03 am, just about the same as yesterday, only earlier, so I lay staring into the ceiling; I pretend it is the clouds I am watching, then the stars, then just a ceiling, which for some reason is far more occupying. I recommend the activity. I watch my white, textured ceiling for as long as I can, but I must move; I need to get out of bed, so I do. Drawing out the process. My morning, nothing more than an endless cycle of groveling steps. I pace myself, so when I am done with my morning routine, I should only have enough hours in the day to complete my tasks and final preparations for tomorrow. I should be swimming in delight at the fact of what is to come tomorrow, but that is not what I face. Tomorrow, how joyous it will be. Today, a cruel sentiment to my lost love, some extensive minutes to flavor my time without my dear. I should not think at all, drown myself in to-do's; the first on the list, 'go to store for travel needs which includes food, candy, drinks, and all else thought up.' Not as early as my normal town entry takes place, but not too late for all the town to be out and about. To Stewart's store I go, not with the car, since it is all fixed up and clean, no, I walk, preserving old-fashioned me. I have employed a much heftier bag of my own that I now use for the store; its workings are marvelous in comparison to the typhoon of groceries I had once experienced. Aisle four, candy galore. I choose for her: gummies, gum, suckers, and some chocolate. Away from the sugar, up to '4B' - potato crisps, crackers, soda pop, and jugs for water. In the store, gathering supplies, I seemed to have forgotten my goal of prolonging time, moving quickly, swiftly about the aisles to check out; I am already on the road, only minutes from where I stood before the retrieving of my groceries. My walk, I must prolong, so for a change, instead of going straight home, I walk the sidewalks of Main Street, peering through the windows as I pass ever so slowly, a barbershop; inside, a man with hair fine-tuning the head of a man with none. The pharmacy, that awkward man in his awkward stance. A dining establishment, is it a diner or a pub? I have always wondered; one side of the wall with empty tables, one with mothers celebrating a day away, another with girls the age of Charlotte laughing at each other's words, and a rugged man behind a counter. Now a bank, no one, of course, just a man in a second-hand kind of suit. Turning the circle, back at Stewart's, and down the road facing home. I would go the back way, but I can't take the face of our willow. Instead, to exert the same use of time, I wave, I stop, I talk to the neighbors, of course, and act as the friendly man I am, at least as they know me to be. At last, I face my drive with my willows, sometimes crying, sometimes wailing in joy, their moods change so it seems with mine. Today they wave in gloom, their branches hanging, and the green not so bright, dew running down like tears. I only face the left side; for the right, I may catch sight of Charlotte or her home, which is not a thing I can do. The time—12:06 pm. From afar, a dog barks, although I'm sure it was a laugh. Every moment, still I move slowly. I collect all the food and books, organize them in the car, and place them in their perfectly accessible location, making the automobile suitable for our travels. I had barely driven in Maine, I have had lots of practice while here, and of course, I am familiar with all of the laws, but I would be entrusting Charlotte with the directions for our journey. At home, she has been very capable with the road-lined papers. Knowledgeable on what route to take, which not to, and she has even memorized major roads where turns take place, but if we drift off into the never-ending foreign roads, she and I alone to fade into the light of day, then I should not complain. With the car packed and only a few hours left of the day, I cook up a meal to pass the time. I eat, staring off to a distant blade of grass, then shower, change, and set out clothes for tomorrow. I read, I dust, anything to make it to the night. And just as I had hoped, in all of my decelerated day, I have made myself tired in how much of a bore this day has been. It had begun raining about twenty-five minutes ago, the perfect sound to put me to sleep. This day, however humiliating, has come to an end; therefore, my wearying ways can forever be put to sleep and long past, for tomorrow is just but a night away, and Charlotte and I will be out in the world together, away from this town, a real couple. Tomorrow it will be. Tonight, I close my eyes, and tomorrow a world awaits.

24

With the rise of the southern sun, its ray's shining brighter than any day before. With no intention of wasting my morning away, and with all the despair, the longing, the wait, the humiliation of my survival skills in her absence, today, this morning, I meet my love again, and we shall ride away. She and I agreed days before that we would waste no time, so I rush, putting on my best nonchalant yet striking look and cleanest shoes. I comb my hair, and down the steps I go, nearly forgetting my watch, like a child I am. I put together our breakfast, which we should eat in the car. Out I am, opening the door, holding my eyes to the car in repetition of my previous days until I realize I no longer must refrain from my glances, so up I look over my majestic field, growing ever more to catch my Charlotte's eyes. We act as we did in our first meeting; how coincidental we should both meet here again. Charlotte, in her best clothes for town, growing as the grass does in the morning sun, shining like a diamond among the trees, a nymph she is in her divine light. Just as our first meeting, my heart seizes to her stare; she waves frantically, beginning to run to me, leaping into my arms— how unexpected, how fulfilling, how preposterous I feel. Could she have jumped just now into my arms? Yes, she could; she did. She is within my arms. My arms are wrapped around her, holding her onto my body. Our parting- the best thing to have been possible for our love. She jumps down and into the car ever so swiftly. I follow, running around the front; she is already seated, grinning uncontrollably, facing forward. I, now seated beside her. In her top, her collarbones lie exposed unintendedly. I watch her breathe as if awaiting terror. She looks to me with her teeth biting her lips, as she is frozen in a cycle of smiles and grins and gleams, unable to convey a word. What had come of Charlotte in the past days? Why this behavior now? She still breathes methodically. Slamming her face to mine, and in the blink of my eyes, Charlotte, who just sat across from has now, just missed my lips. They lie on my cheek, and her hand upon my leg, the other around my neck. A sensation that should not leave me for my summer, I know. How quick she moves, already on her seat with map in hand, smile still on her face. I begin the car, taking off onto our voyage, as she goes over where to go first, second, then third as though I hadn't already heard for days upon days. Her voice, the reason I should not penetrate her discussion, for a man should never interrupt an angel.

Minutes pass, and out of our town we go. Charlotte looks out the window onto the world in such a way that quickens my breath and puts an ache in my heart. She looks out for miles onto fields of grass with cows and small hills. Mile by mile, she smirks, and in her eyes, I can see the joy, but still, she looks as if she is aware of the fires she has cast; she looks at the world in a way you would believe all of it was at her fingertips. How hard it is to drive with her so near and unable to watch her without end. All the books I have packed remain untouched, for her eyes belong to the road and the scenery, that of which she has never once seen. Down the roads, and by the homes, she sings, and dances with her shoulders alone upon the endless country roads. Her anticipation grows and with it my love. And in some of her tunes, she manages to have my voice join in; she sways her head and lets her arm out the window to feel the wind floating her hand up and down. An hour and a half into the ride, the scenery has not changed; she grows tired of the same house and grass on repeat, so it seems, for she picks up a book, reading a word or two, "Would you like to hear?" she asks.

"Your voice? Yes, much better than the quiet."

And so, she reads aloud, "According to Greek mythology, humans were originally created with four arms, four legs and a head with two faces. Fearing their power, Zeus split them into two separate beings, condemning them to spend their lives in search of their other halves." She speaks as Aoede would sing.

In her pause, I speak, "The Symposium, Plato."

"Yes!" Charlotte excites.

I'm well aware of Plato's works; his works on love, quite empathetic toward myself. My search for the other half of me is over. It has been from the moment Charlotte and I's eyes caught the light of one another's. She continues, the more she speaks, the more her words morph into the feeling of a finger, words combining to sentences, her sentences crawling up my leg; word by word, she speeds my breath, sinks my heart, pounds my chest in, until her words can hold me to her captivity no longer, they flee from her tongue like a waterfall. My body gives way to her heavenly pronunciation and rhythm, her tone and poise. The forty-five minutes we had to share gone only in three, so it would seem.

"Athens!" Charlotte exclaims. My hands grip the wheel, veins just beginning to reveal; as Charlotte looks to the town, I must catch my breath.

"Pull over, pull over!" she yells.

Who knew such excitement would give way? Upon arrival, Charlotte lost all sight of her plans and her itinerary. It could have blown out the window, and she would not give as much as a sigh. How happy it makes me to see my Charlotte in such felicity. The town is not much to me, not much like the average one of those North, but to an unimmunized eye, it must be a metropolitan. And how big her eyes have grown. I find a place to park, and she pushes us out of the car, nearly onto the street as soon as I do. On the street corner beside our car, she takes in all that surrounds her; minutes pass, she fully immerses herself into her surroundings until she is out of this first state, then she moves on to check her maps, folds them, then hands them to me, of course, for my pockets to carry. While beginning to walk through the town, she has me at surprise as in the arrival we made just minutes before, it was as if she has never been anywhere in the world, which in technicality is correct. Still, as we move through town, the foreigner, the wide-eyed, naive girl she arrived as has already seemed to have faded. As quick as the moment of our arrival came, she was back to her controlled, effortlessly poised self. She has not a lesson on travel, yet she acts as if she has come here every weekend. I fall behind maybe two steps for her to notice the distance between us; she grabs me forward, and to our first stop, the theater, to a show I stand unaware of, but that she has such a desire to see. Come to think of it, I do not believe she even knows what the picture is; she only knows that this is what she absolutely needed to do. Although she is not fond of sitting, as we just had sat for quite some time, she chose the first showing to be one hundred percent positive that she would sit in an actual theater. I even get her popcorn and a drink to complete her perfect design. With the movie at its end, we waltz to a real ice cream bar. My dearest, amused by the leather seats and the bar where we sit. How kind she is to have saved up enough money to pay for her day. Honestly, where she got it, I have no idea, maybe from watching children. Either way, I cannot let her use her own, and I had no intention of her doing so. This is a matter she should argue over for hours. She does not like me paying, but really, even if I was not simply kind, her being here with me is more of her doing me a favor than what she believes. The theatre, ice cream bar, town shops, park, and Main Street are all much grander than our own. Full of so many colorful people, young ladies and men, tens upon tens of men in suits, maids about, and for Charlotte's utmost excitement, we take an extensive tour of the grandest architecture she has appeared to have seen. We drive to the Chamber of Commerce, which she admires in great length. Then home by home, she passes in awe, marveling at their columns, their large doors, and gardens. To her, Athen's school, the University of Georgia, is a most profound delight. As she watches the students, particularly this young girl and boy, both young and in lustful love, playing together on the recreational field, I watch Charlotte who in comparison is nowhere in relation to that girl or any of the others in the populous around us. Charlotte, a beautiful obscurity, her looks— devilish, young, but entirely illecebrous. Her walk, her talk, and her play are all much older than that of these girls, yet her delight remains in her youth; in her eyes, you can see the fading joy behind the sorrowful stories surrounding her nymphic glee all put together to create what is she. We watch the people, all of them, and in not a single one of the probable one hundred, do I feel any enticement to anyone but my little love.

Our day full of so many stops, so many buildings to see, and still not a moment to breathe it all in. Maybe the "us" would have set in, just maybe if I could have shown her, shown us off to the world. Though, I wonder if nothing could make me as happy as to see my dear smile as so. I grant every wish, every want or need, I complete for her, and I am totally fine in doing so. So happy for this day which may come to a close. With hours gone by, feeling as though only one has done so. Will we leave soon? I do not know. What time was it that Charlotte had to get home? It is nearly sunset, and we have just begun to eat dinner. Quite the fancy place if I should say, but an hour and fifty-seven minutes it should take us to get home, six we finish, home at eight?

We eat. 7:00 pm, home at nine? That should be fine. My darling, transfixed by the servers in black ties and suits with shoes that shine. She tells me she is glad she wore her best clothes. Through dinner she talks to our waiters, practically putting them on a show, but with me, I know, she is driving home. Dessert, I provide her as one last surprise, a tiny chocolate cake and a spoonful of vanilla ice cream and shared to her request. How kind. Although finished, still we sit, talking all about the day, about the city and the people. I think much about the people. Time slips by, for it is already 7:47, home at ten? When should her father be home? Charlotte doesn't seem to mind. We walked all day, so the car may be a mile away or so from our restaurant. We walk on the Athenian road, the moonlight reflecting off the puddles of water upon the street. Streetlights and the faint lights of storefronts line our way. Charlotte and I walk together down the middle of the road, dancing as she slips onto the sidewalk, swinging around a light pole, and running back to me. I mimic her, and she laughs. We conjoin in the road and walk back to the car; this walk, we do not speak, we both are seemingly too enlightened to form a word, so we only walk with an incessant haze surrounding us. To the car, our day almost to an end. How sad it seems to have gone so quickly. In the car at last, I drive home with Charlotte as my director though at night her task increases in difficulty. Two wrong turns, an extra thirty-five minutes. We miss another turn, forty-five minutes past. We must circle back, one hour and two minutes. Another turn, one hour and thirty minutes. Then again, one hour and fifty-seven minutes. Returning home to the town, we arrive two hours and twelve minutes on the road, and finally, we come to our Main Street with only one small light guiding our way. Our ride, though, every moment with Charlotte fulfilling, the driving, exhausting, and so maybe it is only the haze that my weariness instilled, but our town appears to be so sad. Its buildings are painted within a line of somber grey, a tear blue, despair black, and an empty white. The street just does not reflect the moon as bright; what a pitiful sight to see. On my road, down, I slow, to absorb every last second with my dear, turning into my driveway. Charlotte still comes in and out of sleep, with the map in her lap and books to her right and left; next to me, her hand lays. I park next to my porch, reach my hand to grasp her face, holding her chin, her eyes awake, "We are here, my dear."

"Well then, leave me here; I don't want to wake up."

Alas, if she did, her dream would die. But as I do, leaving her only momentarily to make a trip to carry some food inside, a loud truck pulls into Charlotte's drive— her father. I wake Charlotte immediately. She slips out to run to the side of my house, running but four steps and returning to me; she kisses my cheek, only to miss my lips once more. She pushes herself up to her toes in efforts to reach my height, nearly to whisper, "Thank you William.

Thank you, I—" She runs off, fading into the night on the side of my home, her father still trying to make his way to the door in a semi-straight path. I see Charlotte reappear vaguely in the distant light. I watch her as she enters through her window; her father enters the house only moments later. From my porch, I see the windows, filled with light. Suddenly, a bottle I hear breaks, but neither voice nor pain follows. My love, I can only pray if the Lord should even hear what I have to say; Charlotte, I know what you wish to say, Charlotte my dear, my little doe, so sad and grey, yet the nymph you are, in your eyes, lies the pain, I love you. I do, yours truest. Goodnight Charlotte, I whisper to the southern air in hopes the wind from the branches of the willow shall carry it away and make my word's way to her, flooding her mind. As I close my eyes and bring my ears up further into the sky, I can hear her voice, revealing the same.

25

I wake up the happiest man to be in existence. Washing my face, changing only my pants, to be hit with a surge of hunger. I make my way down the steps. In descending, I see a piece of paper below, peering up from beneath the door, halfway finding itself in my home. I quicken my step to reach it, picking it up. On the front, it reads, "To William."

I open the envelope ever so carefully, slowly awaiting whatever may be inside. I read it to you as follows,

"Dearest William,

I have enjoyed our talks, the books, and the walks, but you have taken every second of my life away from me, and for that, I despise you. If I never laid my eyes upon you again, I should die just as happy. Maybe happier. I am leaving. By the time you have read this, I should be gone. I am in Mississippi with my great aunt. I won't tell you anymore because I do not want you here. I'm sorry I ever laid my eyes on you, you took my life away, and I should have it returned. So, William, please don't miss me.

Your 'dear,'

Charlotte"

In the final breath, it took me to read, to search between the lines of her words, to evaluate her phrases, her spaces, and her signature, I have been stabbed from the backside completely unaware, and now fading away— my love, my fire, my sin, my doe, my Charlotte, why must you say all of these words? You make into sentences, line upon line, all of it, lies! I know you would never say; you would never mean anything in this letter. You nearly told me you loved me only hours ago. You love me. I love you. You love me! You do! I promise you do! I feel the blood running down my leg onto my socks then to the floor; I stand in a puddle of my own melancholy. My heart I once felt beat, my heart I know I felt beat just this morning has sunk, to the pitless abyss somewhere within me it has gone. And in not a moment more, I run onto the porch, out to her home, her father's truck gone. I open her window, sticking my head in— no Charlotte. Walking to her front door, through the glass, I peer, and in the distance, I find her mother in her chair. The next window, no one. Nothing, the next window, no movement, no Charlotte, and the next, nothing still, the next, to the next, to the last. No one. Not another living soul. My Charlotte had left. She is gone. How is she gone when she was just in my arms? She was here, and now it is as if she has died. Or have I? Why my soul? Why must her soul be departed from mine? My joy, my light, please, where are you?

Charlotte! I run to our willow, I sit, and I cry. I lay my head back, and I face the sky, but in the clouds, I see her eyes. I face the pond in the distance, and I see us walking in the fog. I face the house, and there we are on the porch. I close my eyes, tears nearly filling them entirely and in all the rumble of emotion, I fall back to sleep, and a spiral swells in my mind. The pressure builds, and into a sleep I go, down the rabbit hole I fall, wiped out by my own emotion, suffocated by tears. With nowhere to even begin a search for Charlotte, she has condemned me. The grasp she has always had, only now stronger in her betrayal. What a man I am to be beneath a willow tree, a face as red as the sunrise. Picking myself up from the ground my heart has just broken upon, I walk back to my home. I walk into my room, to my bed, and for the first day of my life, I shall not leave this bed until the sun rises again.

Only she haunts me in my dreams, I close my eyes and she's still there. Her laugh echoes through my halls. Her voice stains my mind.

Through the procession of sleep, to none, to lying soundless and stale, to tears, to pain, to anger. In a dream, I found myself sitting and reading on my back porch until, looking up from a word, I found Charlotte running across the field from behind our willow with her skirt flying up in the wind and her voice calling out to me so much so that the I felt the vibrations in my ear. I awake from this dream to my most lyrical self; I utter the words only out my window, to the world, for my willow to hear and for the wind to blow:

Oh, my dear, where do you hide?
Is it within the trees,
Or with the bees, or soaking in the sun?
My love, I lost; where can you be?
At the shore? Or out to explore?
Or hiding right here with me?
My love, I am blind.
I only wish to find,
My little love, for you are so divine.
Where can you be?
Are you in the air?
Or only in my prayers?
I just wish to know,
When did you disappear?
Why are you no longer here?

Have I even spoken, or do I stay still within my dream? Either way, I wish for an angel to hear what I have to say, and maybe, the Lord shall take pity and bring Charlotte back to me. How long can a bed hold a man? I wonder, how long would it take to lose use of my legs if I should never get up again? Just this morning all of the sorrow I had lost in the sight of Charlotte, flooded me once again, and all the anguish and pain returned to my bloodstream. Only now have I been given a taste of such joy that living in such despair feels incomparably darker. My first day, with my love lost, and I, too with her, lost in my own halls, my own home, lost to the decay of my heart. Goodnight my reader. I cannot bare to continue. Goodnight Charlotte, wherever you may be.

26

Three days since tragedy. I cannot bring myself to move, let alone write. Shall I go on? What more is there to say? Charlotte is gone. I've spent these days with only my soundless mind, desolate, though this is fine because I rather only be accompanied by silence than the noise of memories or the screams of thoughts. Though every day at some peculiar time, the soundlessness turns to a stabbing pain, out of nothing, some demon creeps up from behind and holds me in a mix of pain and confusion until it leaves me with only a ringing in the ears. I believe I could say after three days of the institutional feel that having movement in my hands should constitute a sign of healing.

There are only twenty-four hours in a day, 1,440 minutes, and 86,400 seconds, yet somehow, a single day feels to last the length of three. It is past lunch, I did not eat, but I walked to the kitchen. I'm in the study now; I face the condemnation of Charlotte's seat on my chair, her gum in my top drawer, her face in the bookshelf. I cannot but throw myself back into my soundless abyss, so I throw myself into a book. Yes, the endless series of words flood and replace the thought that may linger before it. Where should I go, Greece, Rome, France, Britain? Anywhere from here. I understand as a man, I should not have the longing to run to a home, but at this moment, there is an aching desire within me to go back to my aunt, back to her home, and rock with her in that salty breeze. I hadn't known what it was like before Charlotte; I had never danced in the rain, never walked barefooted through a field. What was my life before her? Work, my aunt, talk of work, the news, what more? I should despise Charlotte as well. She grants a man life, then tears it away from him and leaves him less than he was before, sinking down a slow spiral into the Hell flames which danced within her eyes. Perhaps I should try another book, attempt another escape. I shall try Germany.

27

A night not in my bed, a morning to myself in a separate room away from my encapsulant, but a morning that has me awake to Charlotte's image sitting in my desk chair across the room. Was it all just a dream? Had I only fallen asleep with Charlotte in my home, and had I awoken to her dandelion face still in love with me? I believe I hear her speak, her foot taps against my desk, which her legs are propped upon, her body slouched back into my chair, the window above my desk open, and a few strands of her hair fly up every minute or so. Her face lit to a golden ray in the sun. What is it she has just said?

"What a beautiful day!"

Oh, my dear, I knew you wouldn't have left me. I knew it wasn't true! "Yes. Charlotte, it is very nice indeed." I exclaim. She props her body up further as she slides into the chair too deep. Turning the page of her book, I reposition myself to come to a seat, "How long was I asleep, Charlotte?"

"Oh, not too long; I don't know, an hour or so."

"Is that right? How strange."

"Strange?" she whispers ghastly.

"Charlotte?" I get up to put my book on the shelf, I hear her speak again, but the wind gets in the way, "What was that you said, Charlotte?"

"Hm?" she responds.

"What did you say. I didn't hear you."

She sits too close to the window, but still, she speaks again, "How is it that your only friend is a high school girl? Huh, William?"

I expect a laugh, but no, she remains stone-cold. My face immediately moves from the shelf to her face by the window. I walk to her to take her hand, "Charlotte, I have more friends. What mood is this that you are in?"

Her eyes appear glazed by an odd coldness she did not usually possess. She moves her eyes to the desk, and mine follow to spot the letter lying just as it had in the dream; looking down upon her words, I read again,

"Dearest William,

I have enjoyed our talks, the books, and the walks, but

....

William, please don't miss me.

Your 'dear,'

Charlotte"

I look up to her eyes, but she is no longer there. My hand which had held hers just seconds ago, lies frozen in the air, empty and cold. What mockery, what fun the Lord is having, what he is pitting onto me for all that I have sinned! How funny my highness can be! What pawn, what joker in the play I have come to be. No. No, that's not it. You, my Lord. You are on my side; I know you were just trying to speak to me like all those crazy Baptists say you do. Yes, you are telling me that the town thinks I only spend my time with Charlotte. From an outsider, that can't look good. I'm supposed to be their lawyer; what must they think of me? Today's itinerary must change! First, go to the market, then to the office, to the shops, talk along the way, repeat this every day. What must they think I do with this girl, that I am some sort of deviant! They would kick me out or burn me for that, their own lawyer put to trial, with who to persecute, or that piece they may skip entirely and send me straight to the ultimate judge there is. I have to find a woman! I must establish a connection! This is what I must do.

Anna Street – Brunette, roughly five foot two, with a hideous face in disguise behind a semi-appealing shape.

Hannah May - More southern accent in her than she is in the South.

Eloise Snyder - Name as horrendous as she; moles all across her face, probably a chest full of hair.

Louisa Brown - A schoolteacher, obnoxiously tall, but not too skinny or too large, a brunette, who dresses dark, on the paler side, and an accent that may be just so bearable. Husband— dead. Good with kids. Away all day for her work.

The list of single women in this town could extend, but I believe, she should do. She has complimented my accent before, and maybe it was in her tone, but she was, in fact, a bit of a flirt. At least, I know she finds me appealing, to say the least. Her house is only a bit away from mine in between the path to the main store. She is in my direct line; maybe, if I am lucky, she will be outside today on my trip to the store. No, I should go to the court to check in, talk to everyone, make a good appearance, then take a look around, open some doors for people, sit with the old women on the benches, and ask them about their dogs or whatever other frivolous things are in their lives. I've learned in attending church of the promise to Charlotte that pride is a sin, and so, I do not wish to sin, but I must say I am an attractive man. I am tall, six foot three in preciseness, with darker blonde hair, brown, you could say in certain light, soulful eyes, strong hands, and my accent, of course, more apparent than ever in the South. A female companion for publicity purposes should come of ever most ease, most definitely in this town. Now, if I begin to people-please, to small talk, to baby kiss, I should become the most appealing man to these women's sight. Now I must decree. Besides, there is no time for talk of myself when I must embark on a most imperative mission to save my own image from the scrutiny of the public eye. These things you must watch for as a public servant, you know. In fact, for an extra fee, there was a class at my law school entitled, "How to Get Away with Murder and Other Atrocities," looking back, I should have paid the fee. Though I doubt the matter of having a town believe you not to be psychotic in your choice of affection may not have been discussed. In my banter, I've already walked out the door, down the street, two houses, three, four, six, eight. No sign of Louisa; I wonder if people call her Lou? I don't linger; I shouldn't make myself into a stalker as well. The ninth house, no one. The tenth, no one. On Main Street, no one still. Darn. It's Sunday, the time, 10:27 am. Run William, before those heavy doors close and you are cast out for all eternity! In my shoes, to hell already in the mud; the price you pay, I presume to meet sainthood. Wonderful, I can slip in just unnoticed enough, but of course, Louisa stands right where Charlotte used to; in fact, as I come in, I am sure she is Charlotte, but then the light adjusts. Louisa sings in the choir as well. I promised Charlotte that I would attend church every Sunday, and though I made the promise to keep her in church and her instinctively in love with me, it appears somehow, I am drawn to keep my word. Would I have been here if I had remembered it was Sunday and had not a plan to win a woman? I believe maybe by Charlotte's overarching power and everlasting grip I would have brought myself here. Charlotte, how your hair glows, and how your white lace brings out your tan legs and your eyes. Charlotte, my dear, where did you go?

"Amen Church!" I am interrupted.

"Amen!" the church chimes in unison.

The pastor sings as his ensemble echoes. My eyes reach Louisa's once more. Erasing something as divine as my Charlotte, won't ever be a task I should call easy.

Grueling sermon—you live, you die, but still, you live in everlasting peace and love. How can one live past death in peace and love when you couldn't but experience the pleasure while in life; it is all but a ruse.

There Louisa stands with her school children and their mothers; how darling she can be. Somehow, I feel my feet below me, moving in her direction, a smile making itself apparent. Making room on my face, an opening for words to free themselves, "Hello, children," I say. Hello children? Why, why must I say this? "So, I am William, the new guy in town. I was wondering, what are some of your favorite things to do around here? I figure I could use some advice." There we go, what a charm I forgot I could be.

"Getting ice cream!" one chants.

"Walking the river!" goes another.

"Playing with my dogs," another.

"Building things," adds yet another.

One curious child chimes, "Where are you from? You don't sound much like us." Quite perceptive he is.

"I moved here from Maine, but I was born in a nation named England. Have you learned where that is?"

Louisa works herself into the conversation with a great gleam, "They have. They have just learned to read their maps, haven't you all?"

"Yes, Ms. Brown..." The children draw, all still with a tint of joy. They seem to like her and I, too, apparently.

Louisa takes notice, "Hi, I am Louisa Brown, the teacher here. How are you liking the town?"

"I'm William, the lawyer. It is quite quaint to say, very eclectic, but the words 'largely petite' come to mind." She laughs. I can make her smile; what a swoon I am to be already. Her laugh holds a familiar tone, one melody it seems I have heard a time or two. How can such an angel have such a demonic presence in her absence? She's gone; it is Louisa who is here; William, get yourself through this, "Louisa, would you care to take a walk with me and tell me more about the town and you?"

"That would be darling!"

She smiles softly and yet again, another familiar phrase, although she appears to use it without the mockery. We begin to walk, and immediately she travels towards the path that Charlotte and I would take. I divert her immediately to the main strip so that she could show me her favorite shop; this is what she hears at least, the real reason being I had, at this moment, come to believe it was not my dear Charlotte who had been haunting me, but Louisa who had spied and figured out my nymphet's laugh and phrases, who had observed our walks. She is perhaps the embodiment of jealousy; it is her who is the problem; how could I go on with this charade? How may I pretend to be fond of Ms. Louisa, midlife crisis, teen wannabe? Maybe just a bit longer until my presence would be enough, or perhaps just a singular "date" to throw everyone off course, but then I will feel the need to devote myself only to my work, and any romantics would distract me too much. Yes, what a brilliant man I am. A plan stitched with perfection.

To catch you up, we are still walking; she has shown me her favorite place, the flower store. How original. She told me she was, 'dazzled by our walk' but needed to get home to draft lesson plans. A woman who uses the word dazzled is one who holds a discountenance. Regardless, I let her off to her lesson plans. Now, with still a day to fill,

I shall make my way to the court to observe my office, examine my bookshelves, and perhaps any future cases. The court is quite a lovely building, standing tall and white with columns and etchings, words in Latin engraved. How the court came to be, I am completely unaware; seeing the rest of this town, I doubt there is not a single man who can even read Latin within four states on all sides of ours. Regardless of how its beauty may have come to be, I am grateful to have such a place at least adorned with opulence. A gem amongst the rough, my pearl in this denim town. Charlotte had once said she loved the courthouse; she would sit on its steps and read, and when she did, she would be looked at as if she was crazy. No one could see her beauty like me.

Thankfully, being Sunday, I have no employees to meet; therefore, I am led to my office, which I hadn't seen before today, by the police chief alone to find two floor-to-ceiling bookshelves that should have adequate space for my things. Although, as the chief has informed me, I have learned that the police work from within the courthouse, this is how I have come to meet Adam, a gruesome-looking man, muscular and brute. I don't think he has much of a care for me; he seems sickened at the admiration shown by the townspeople toward myself. He sees himself (a police officer) as the only form of hierarchy. I most previously despised men who appeared as he, but of course, he didn't stay in my office long, for he has much better to distract himself with.

Somehow, I stared at those office walls of mine to be for what felt to be a millennium. It feels as though all I have heard is a clock ticking, counting my time left on earth, my clock of life perhaps. Each tick, a ring of despair, clenching the pain in my heart. My office being so empty provides me a scene no different from my home. I can't take it; I must go, say my goodbyes, and alert whoever of the police force I may find that they should be expecting me more often and that I am extremely pleased with the facility.

Now the walk home, the remainder of my melancholy as the wind laughs at each step I take, the sun my spotlight to some sad show. A few children go by every now and then on their bicycles or running by with their soccer balls. Some ladies in their gardens, some men mowing their lawns. Waving becomes exhausting, so I look forward to my walk alone, only with the willows to wave their leaves to me. In my dejection, as I look to the willows so sad and weeping, I wonder exactly for why should a willow weep? If all that it is given in life is the sun and the moon, the clouds, and the rain, if all it has to see is pure and beautiful? For why should a willow weep if it may watch a kiss, a kid, a dog, or even just a frog? Does the willow weep for a child who has fallen? A dog who is lost? A woman who has been hurt? A man who has lost his love? The child, the dog, the woman, and the man all look to the willow in awe of its beauty, so why should a willow weep? Maybe I know. The willow weeps for its soul is more beautiful than anything on earth that it may find, and so it weeps for the child and the frog and the dog that it cannot help. Its roots keep it alive while trapping it to the ground. Its branches only allowed to move in the direction of the wind, and its bark unable to speak. I wish the willow only knew it does not need to speak or curse its roots, that standing there alone with its swinging leaves, it gives a child strength, a woman love, and a man hope; its sadness is a bearer of joy to the world. Don't weep, willow.

I come to my front porch again, another lonely walk to lead me only to you, my lonely steps where Charlotte once accompanied me a time ago. I should not wait at my door any longer for someone I know will not be opening the door for me to come in; I may be locked out for eternity if I do so. It is already 6:00 pm, so today, I shall just eat and lead myself to sleep, for Hell shall begin again with the light of the sun.

28

Another day, another attempt at productivity. I have gone to the store and the courthouse, but practically nothing more. Today, around noon, as I stood in an aisle looking for bread, I heard a girl laugh. I had heard Charlotte. I grabbed the first loaf available and followed the music; I came to the back of a girl who stood at her height, and with hair of Charlotte's exact color, she turned her left knee into her right, and at that moment I knew my angel had returned to me. A man, three aisles behind me called for her; she passed me with a vacant grin, and in her eyes was nothing but innocence, a world away from anything of my dear. I tried to forget the incident, I believed I had, but as I walked from the court by a near 4:00 pm, the end of my day, a girl was running away with hops so familiar as she turned to the sun's rays which had covered her face, I was certain this must be her, but then the sun had faded and so with it my muse. I walked, my typical path to my willows, still in silence but accompanied by serenity. I thought maybe hope had come through, but when unlocking my door, some force so strong turned my head to Charlotte's home, and I felt I had seen her ghost coming from the door, uttering those exact words from our first encounter. The bullets of euphoria she had once used to shoot me down had become bullets of metal as they were designed to be, each only causing pain, a silent pain that, like the bullet of metallic would kill me slowly but inevitably. Why must an angel fall onto a man who loved her like his god?

29

It has been two days. I have been struck once more with the intense pain of lifelessness, to which I have entered a state of sorrow. I haven't slept as much as one would think; I only lay contesting my empty wall with my emptier gaze. I turn to my other side, but there on that wall is the window that looks onto Charlotte's home, and so I turn again, and maybe by just an illusion, on occasion I feel some drop of dew slide from my eye, down over my nose, onto my cheek to its landing place on my sheets. I do not remember thinking a single thought in these two days, but then again, I do not remember whether I had even blinked. My sense has returned to the extent that I can move my pen again. The pain in my body, you see, isn't sharp, no, it is not like a knife, but not much like a suffocation, maybe an ache? I do not know what this is, this feeling, this strange possession of my soul. What poison is this? I do not understand. Did it seep through the dirt? Or into my water? Had it become mixed with the river? Is it in the air? Does it move with the branches of the willow? Had I breathed it in as I stepped foot into this town, or was it from Charlotte's breath I had breathed in as she got close? Maybe it is not a poison; I do not feel it in my veins, but only in my heart, no, not in, wrapped around, holding it tight, pulling my chest in, and never letting it make an escape. Escape, is that what I should do? Escape to my Lord? From this world? I should have stayed in the abyss. It was much quieter; the lack of thought may just be better than the cascade. What is the time? Half past nine? I'll let myself think this is so, for I can go to sleep and no longer think. Let me not drown myself tonight. Perhaps something will come of the morning, who knows.

30

Maybe three days away from the world have been enough? I shall re-immerse myself; I will tell everyone I have been very busy with my home duties. I should have just created an entirely new life for myself when I came to this town because it seems I have made up enough lies that I could live off of them if only they were transferable to coins. I need to look as presentable as possible, as put together and neat as a man can; I must defend my reputation button by button in hopes everyone will believe I spend so much time away in such clever mystery, so much so that I am titled the arcane man. Out the door, but today in no rush, with no life to build, no story to write for myself, just an average man on a stroll, more average than the next. To the court I go to say hello, and then to stop at a shop, maybe two. Just making it onto my porch, and in the corner of my eye, I watch Charlotte as she runs into her home. Turning immediately only to find nothing, no one on the porch, not the sound of the door closing, not even a sign of movement in her home. I haven't but stepped off my porch, and still, she haunts me. I look up to the sky, up to the bluebirds singing their sad songs, to the clouds so far away, to the ones that look like Charlotte's eyes, and then I look away to the trees as their branches blow, to the mailbox rusted and grey. How sad life is; how long shall this go on? To town, to civilization, to other souls. Today I run through the stores, to the post office, and to the flower shop to see Louisa. At last, I have reached the court. The sheriff tells me that I am not to start my work until September and that I have been coming into the office too often. He has turned me away! And away I go into a lost space; he is right but what am I to do? There are only so many doors to open in this town, and all the grass to explore, I once walked with Charlotte. I cannot bring myself to walk it again.

"No, I'm not supposed to be in school; it is summer break!" I hear my darling's voice, her remarks just as they would have been weeks ago, the same strawberry blonde. It is her! I know.

"Charlotte, you've returned!" I call out, with the return of not even a glance.

The flower shop's owner takes the girl by the hand, and they walk away. It had to have been her, but Paul does have a daughter; maybe it wasn't, but it had to have been her voice. I go home before I have the chance to find Charlotte in the emptiness anymore for the day. She is becoming louder, I fear, more apparent; I can taste her breath in the air. Maybe I shouldn't stay here. Perhaps I should move again, have a complete renewal in a town anew, yet again where I will not even dare to peer at a young girl once more so that I may go on to live. But Charlotte may return and if I am gone, she should never find me. I must stay until the day I may see her face again.

A way to distract myself from the monstrosity in which I call my life is to clean. Since I have been at my home far less than usual, my office has accumulated a desk of discombobulated papers stacked tall and finished by a fine layer of dust, books which have been left overturned upon nearly every surface, a window hidden to me covered in a mass amount of dirt on its exterior, and a floor in desperate need of vacuuming. Though my bedroom remains exquisitely bear, it is, too, in probable need of deep cleaning. I work just as I tell you the tasks: organize papers, clean up books, put the place into a sort of order once again, vacuum, clean the window, and dust within the mix. There, my office is returned to its previously appealing state, but now I find myself sitting at my empty, large table, praising the time I have passed but re-envisioning my happiest self, my dream-filled days. I look through my glass doors, the glass like a haze, behind it holding a scene of a young girl and a man completely in love yet doomed from their start. Time to clean my room I believe.

31

On a night typical to any other, I lay in my hard bed upon wrinkled sheets with only insomnia to accompany me. After about three hours of sleep, I awake again. Tonight, in routine, I stare at my ceiling faintly lit by the moon. Out from the complete silence, is that an impatient knocking? But not upon my door surely, the sound is as if it is on glass. It must be the limbs of a tree, an animal, or simply the wind upon the glass. Maybe if I just shut my eyes. There, the sound again! The knock has grown more impatient, and its fists have become faster and its pressure harder. Although, it is not as though I was sound asleep, and with nothing at all to do, I should investigate. Up I go from my bed, feeling my way with my hands through the hall down the stairs, the sound just as I had thought, not from the front door. Louder it grows, and still ceaseless, the sound not from the great room, not from my office. A possibility, though, are the large windows back in the study. The sound louder but still muffled, not here either. Through the door, into the kitchen, out through the glass doors, I look and nothing, but the noise is at its loudest. Another addition— some muffled puzzling tune. Forgetting about my kitchen's other window to my left, I go, and alas, the wrist finally in vision, the culprit at reach. Slowly I step sideways just to gain a view. I stop first; with my days as a spy long gone, apparently as the knocking discontinued and the hand flew away. Only seconds and in my glass doors, beyond all belief, stands Charlotte. I have become overwhelmed by familiarity, my heart soaring to its heavens, her bullets shot once more, my jaw dropped, my eyes nearly producing a tear. For weeks she has been gone, and now she is here, a dream? This can't be for I never went to sleep. In my absence of movement, she points to the lock, and I let her in.

"William! Oh, William! I'm back; I'm home!" Charlotte rejoices as she leaps into my arms, her attempt to find my lips sending a tingling sensation about my spine. Her demon eyes reflect her understanding of the extent to her welcome exhorted. Though, in a strange sudden change, I throw Charlotte off me.

"Charlotte, no, you left me. You wrote me that note, and you told me you did not want me. You never did, that I ruined you. You must leave! You cannot do this to me now!" I sound.

"William, what letter?" She seems of honest confusion. Yet she only provides me three words after taking minutes as it is to wrap her mind around how to speak.

"What letter? Charlotte, you wrote it! You signed your very name to the thing!" I feel as though I have lost control of my voice.

"I don't know what you mean!" She seems unsure and nearly scared of me. She backs herself into the corner away from me.

"Ok, then, let me show you!" I reign myself in to control myself for her. She stays in the kitchen, away from all windows and the possibility of any light. In my office, I search for the note, hidden beneath some books in a drawer away from my daily sight, but in a place, I know dear. "Here you are." I hand her the paper for her eyes to read.

In the greater silence, she finally looks up, her eyes this time and for the first time, filled with tears; she looks at me, into me, as she always had. She speaks softly, holding back her tears as best she can, "William, I don't know who wrote this. I didn't, I didn't write this." She takes a few moments to further recollect, then she tells me, "I promise. I didn't do this; none of this is even true." I, unsure of what to say, just stare to her soft, sad eyes. "Where did you get this?" she asks.

"I got the letter about three weeks ago; it was slid through my door. Charlotte, if you didn't write this letter, then why did you leave? What happened?"

"My father, you see, he was upset. He noticed how much time I spent with you and decided to send me to my grandma's house. While I was there, she died and my dad knows, but he doesn't know that I came back. My bus was set for two days after tomorrow, Saturday, but I learned that all you do when you are pretty is ask the man working the line if you can exchange your pass for earlier, I told him my dad was real sick and needed me, and well he let me go on no questions asked, then I got back, snuck through town, and now I am here with you, where I will hide."

Having finished her story, "And the letter?" I ask again.

"I never gave it to you; I was forced off. I cried for days; here, wait, I can prove it to you. Give me paper and a pen!" she demands excitedly. She picks up the pen and begins to copy the exact letter onto the paper; she finishes by signing at the bottom. "Here, look, you must look!" Pushing the letters into my face. And in just one glance, the differences are clear. It appears as if someone had attempted her writing, even the foraging of her signature. "It had to have been my father, I know." she interrupts. Tears begin to form in her eyes again. As I turn to her without any words, I continue to draw the silence, pulling it further and further until, "Please, William, I didn't write this, I—" She listens to what she is about to say, and she rethinks. She meant to say she loves me. I know; I can see the words in her eyes.

"Charlotte, I know you did not write this letter." I pause. "I missed you dearly," I tell her.

"You don't know how I've missed you." Her typical smile has finally made its return. Her happiness has found its way into our lives once again. At this moment, looking into her eyes, onto her grin, I realize she is the love I have been looking for all along, every minute, every second, every breath of air. The love I have been looking for in every item and person that belongs to this earth. It was only in finding her that I realized I had always been looking. And in her absence did I realize how much I would be looking. In her absence, every laugh I heard I morphed into hers; every girl afar from behind was a hope of Charlotte's return, but as I moved to face the girl's eyes, they changed from your blue to her brown and my hope of you was gone. When I first came to Georgia, there was an immediate feeling, from my first steps into this town, a feeling as if it were crawling up my leg and spine, sending whispers through my ear, but the softest kind of whisper, almost too faint to hear. The feeling— nearly intoxicating. Still today, it is. The sensation was as if it cleansed me of my melancholy and ended my dissolution, a sort of magic or poison, one so strong it is as if it was found in the roots of the willows or in the planks of my home. In these past weeks, my melancholy returned to me; it found its way home, there was no near intoxication, like the willows stopped swinging. I learn this evening in June, a month almost two from my new beginning, that it is not Georgia; it is another girl, her name—Charlotte. She is the poison in the summer air.

32

In a complete array of emotions, too many to process at once, I am forced with the obstacle of what to do with Charlotte, who was sent away for showing a stronger emotion to me than to her father. She cannot be found here, not even seen. But for the first time in weeks, I have been blessed by my little love once more, and I most absolutely cannot lose her again. Yet, any plans of taking her away, leaving this house and running across the nation, or hiding her here and only letting her out in the night not to be seen should corrupt my legal standing. So, now I face a large moral question to which I should, as any sane man would choose to do, rightfully return her to her home. Yet as she stands in front of me, with her eyes of sky blue that capture the light, she reflects to me the image of my love who has just returned to me. Her bare legs, her stomach, the partial tears down her face. I wish to disregard whatever morals may exist all to be with her. For her, that is it! Yes, I may keep her in my safety, for can

I trust returning her to her father? Or is this argument invalid due to my provocative predisposition for my dear? At this moment, Charlotte and I have sat blankly, staring at one another, her anticipating my decision, but not obnoxious, no, she sits, without a single noise, in silence as we both gaze blankly. Finally beyond both our beliefs, "Charlotte. I must return you to your father. You can come back to me, but if I do anything other than this, the lawyer could be under prosecution and what a speedy trial that would be."

Charlotte does nothing; she doesn't move her legs, or her hands, she doesn't even look up at me; I nearly speak out again, but she finally speaks, "I know, I know, truly, what was I thinking? I know I have to go back, but we can't just leave your house; if he spotted me, he would kill you and drown me, and if you return me directly to him, we will both be shot in the head quicker than we could say I love you."

Reader, oh, reader! I do not tell stories that are untrue. Indeed, Charlotte has spoken the previous words, she spoke them to me, they fell off her tongue and that is what she said! It must mean she loves me. She has tried and tried to say it.

"I will go then." she interrupts my thoughts.

"Charlotte, I wish there was a way for you to stay. It is all I want, but I have not been able to find one solution. Charlotte, please return to me." I tell her.

"I will be here first thing in the morning. Anyhow my father will think I have lots of friends to see just to reassure them I'm still alive, you know." She smiles, but her glee begins to fade just as she walks to the door. With a creak which she tried to silence by sliding out through just a few-inch gap, she slides into the night, turning to the right and jumping down the side opposite, facing her own home to then take the longest route through a thin layer of trees around to the main road where she walks past my driveway to hers. She turns down the long desperate, forsaking road with lost eyes, though she knows exactly where to go. As she walks through those woods and down the road, I can not see her, but instead, I listen to every step she takes to know where to position my eyes from between that slight gap she left in the door. There is just enough room for my head to turn as she turns down her path. As she walks down her own drive, I wonder who may be more nervous, her or I? Step by step, I can hear her breath carried in the wind as it shudders near her porch's steps; up she goes. One, two, three, and there she stands in front of the very door I first saw her appear out of. Only her skin is not glowing in the sun but reflecting a broken porch light, her hair not blowing but filled with dirt from the trees, and a voice non-rapturous but in doom. Her hand, she tries to lift it, only moving an inch, shaking unbearably as it slowly climbs an invisible rope to its final destination; knock, she goes. Once, not loud enough, twice, and a third.

A loud angered voice, "Who the hell is here now?" A terrifying, familiar voice.

The door flings open, "Dad?" she quivers, trembling alone with just a word.

"Charlotte, how in the world did you get here. Why are you here?" he shouts.

"Grandma died, and you, you did nothing, no letter, no showing up, nothing at all. I waited! I waited, and still nothing! I didn't know, maybe you moved, and you didn't know? Maybe you died too? I had to come home! How could I have stayed there? How? You wanted me to waste away there. You, you didn't want me to burden you once again!" she screams at him, somehow in the moment finding the strength to protest his horrid existence.

"Charlotte." His voice sounding strangled, as if he couldn't find the words. And in just one movement alone, he pulls her into his home.

And here, my heart falls completely into some dark rabbit hole. I whisper without realizing, "Charlotte?" To the porch, I relocate to hear every word, none of which could be understood. Maybe it has been ten minutes or twelve? The voices grow much louder, and to my consternation, a gunshot. A gun? A gun! I can't help, so it seems but shed a tear. I run. I jump over that porch's fence, and I run. I run down into the grass; I run to her, to her window, throwing a rock and smashing it open. I see her in her doorway, thank God, my blessed angel hasn't been harmed. My dearest darling, no, she isn't hurt. I get her to look my way, opening the window for her to escape. She runs to me, through the window, and into my arms, providing her a moment of safety.

Completely in tears, she wails, "My mom! My mom! He killed my mom! He— he tried to shoot me, he killed her! She's dead!"

"Charlotte, we must run!" And so, we do. To the nearest neighbor, we run through the willows to find the road, and there we confess to a Mr. and Mrs. Johnson, "Please, her father has just shot her mother, get the police immediately! He is after Charlotte now!" I demand. I stay behind, holding Charlotte as we watch them go. She cannot barely breathe, her tears, lodged inside of her. She shakes completely. I lock her in my arms. I tell her she will be ok, but I don't know if she can hear me, if she can hear anything at all other than the sound of the gun. I know all I can hear is the sound of her scream, ringing and ringing in my ears. Maybe a minute or an hour has passed, not a single tear has dried, but the police just now arrive and off we go. A circus and we are the lion tamers. Her father not tough to hunt as he has barely left his home, there we find him wobbling down his drive. The police almost thinking he shot himself in the leg because of how he drags. In taking longer than we anticipated for him to notice us, he, upon realization screams, "William, William, I'm going to kill you, William! I'm going to poke your eyes out so that you can watch yourself get shot in the head! I swear to you! I swear to you, you son of a bitch!"

The police assume they can now chime in. I do not know what their wait was for; I believe it must've been that they did not want to cut into the madman's monologue! I say not a word to him. He stands there numb. The alcohol has seemed to put every part of his body to sleep with the only thing going being his mouth. This makes him easy to disarm, immediately they get him down. I pull Charlotte to the side, attempting to get her away as her father interrupts, feeling the need to speak once more, "I hope you both rot in Hell."

In the mess we have landed ourselves in, in the middle of the flashing lights, the men in uniforms, the neighbors coming to view the charade, her mom being carried out of the house, Charlotte's head laid upon my chest without any words, this is understandable, but bizarrely no tears. She has run dry. She cannot even get herself to cry.

Our two homes, Charlotte's and mine, the ring. The neighbors, our spectators. Police, our ringmasters. I, the tamer, her father, the lion, and my dear, the little lamb. I have tamed the lion, and now our spectators have nothing more to view; all that's left remains the ringmasters and the lamb.

33

There, Charlotte and I are taken to what the town calls the station, but it is really just a room added onto the courthouse. Police frantically work all about; who knew we had so many? I believe they must have been called in from other towns. While most of them continue to scramble about, one asks Charlotte what occurred, and I, he asks the same. We comply with every bit of direction and answer every question, no matter how frivolous. Despite all that has happened to her, Charlotte must explain the situation in its entirety, and additionally, her family line for the officers to determine who to give her to. The officers have so far collected the following facts: The girl's mother: no siblings, dead parents. The girl's father: no siblings, dad long deceased, and mom just recently departed. Conclusion: no aunts, no uncles, no grandparents, no more siblings, recently departed mother, one living parent newly incarcerated for life (as soon to be determined guilty). The police and anyone to read said report would understand Charlotte is entirely alone, and her life has been encapsulated by death. What are they to decide? This is my urging question. I can hear the indistinct chatter behind the partition walls the officers have set up for themselves— the shuffling, the carelessness at this point in the night; it is all piling up, but to me, I am only accompanied by the deepest heart-swallowing pain, shaking within, scared to know the answer to what will become of us. I cannot even force myself to turn my head to Charlotte, for if I do, I know my tears will begin to drown us all in an instant.

"Charlotte." a deep, grizzly voice whispers, the speaker emerging from behind the wall, "Whose home do you wish to be adopted into?"

In all of my inclinations, had I ever guessed this to be the question asked by these officers. Surprising as could be, but bless small towns and their flexibility concerning the law and procedure. Despite my desire to hear her answer, I still cannot face her, now not out of pity, but fear. Still, I don't get to hear her answer, for we all remain in utter silence as we wait until all the noise in the room turns to a soft shifting. Finally, I turn to see her index finger pointed at me, and following behind, she sounds, "William's." She says, almost forgetting to add the 's' in expressing possession, adding the letter seconds after finishing the pronunciation of my name. A deep sigh lets go from me without my awareness of the action.

"Can you tell us why you would like to go with him?" the same officer asks.

She lingers only momentarily, "Well, he has been my only real friend. He helps me solve my problems and gives me jobs so I can stay away from my home, and he teaches me things about laws and ethics and such to help me have a better future. Maybe I'm not the most credible source on how a father should behave, but I know William is much more than the one I have.... Had." she finishes.

The officers are convinced I know; they usher me not just behind the wall but outside, "William, she has no family, and she is sure she wants to be in your care, so we know, and you know the rules are that we take her until you are processed as the new guardian, but we are all willing to bend the rules. After what she's gone through, we don't want her in some dingy establishment or cell with us. What are a few days? Alright? Of course, unless there are any objections? We know it's a real big thing to ask."

I respond, "No, sir, none at all. I believe in your compassion for the girl. Wherever she could be placed, if I were to neglect, would be another incredible burden for her. I will do my best to help her in this horrific time."

He smiles at me so sincere, as if lost in my affection for her, "Good man, William. Good man. Wait here, and I'll have the guys bring her out."

"Thank you, officer; you, too, are a good man."

Just as promised, minutes have passed, and Charlotte appears. The officers walk her down the steps, but as soon as her second foot touches the ground, she can't help but to assume a sprint, landing on my side. One last time I say,

"Thank you, officers." You see, you must be very polite, exponentially polite to the men who decide your future. As the men turn their backs towards us and take flight up the court's steps, I pull Charlotte in just as she had wished and walk her forward to not only mine, but our home.

In my waking moments, would I ever have imagined the events of the evening and the divine fortune of my nighttime. Charlotte and I walk in silence until we reach a point on our path where no streetlights or homes can identify us in the night. Charlotte utters in the midst, "You know, at the station, when I talked to them about you. Well, you are not like a father to me at all. Maybe it's because I don't know what a real father is, but I know I love you more than I could have ever loved the father I was given."

In my serenity, I realize in her expression that this walk for her is not as it is for me; the peacefulness and joy I feel, she reflects through dejection and mourning. Though I should be wrapped up in her confession, the feeling of remorse settles in, calming my emotions enough for me to compose the line, "You and I, though very different, have no family, that is until we found each other. My dear, I am sure you know my love for you is larger than the willows—" She grins, the sadness in her eyes melting into the slightest of a sparkle, with the willow being her favorite tree; she couldn't but help react as she did in glee despite her present disposition. I attempt to draw up solemness for sympathetic effect, but I have never been much of an actor. We walk up the drive, a walk done by her and me time after time, and yet this walk reminds me of my very first since I had met Charlotte; the day I met her, after coming home later that evening when there was no more misery in the misty air, and I was fully complete. Now here I am again, accompanied by the same feeling. Sadly, I cannot speak the same for Charlotte. I look over to her every few steps to her eyes dropped down and to the tears which fall singularly down her cheek. As we succumb to the very foot of the moonlit porch, she takes one look over to her house, and in succeeding such an action, the look on her face is one that shall be ingrained in me forever—her eyes full of terror, her lips trembling, her breath more of the gasp for air, her collarbone rising each moment she feels she grows closer to strangulation. I see into her mind, replaying the night like a broken record, the grim music singing songs in her head. She stares, remaining trapped in the exact moment; I grab her by the waist with one hand, the other taking her head and placing it onto mine to save her from the horrors of the night. I whisper quietly, in hopes she may not hear, "She loved you very much, I believe it."

What is this, an instant wetness upon my shirt? She has heard.

The night has continued to creep forward, but I feel as though time had stopped. Just as I get Charlotte inside and settled, the sun begins to peek over the trees in the distance. It couldn't already be morning. Though this night felt like a million years to get through, looking back now in the safety of my home, I feel as if I have just blinked, but what is time if not confusing. I ask if

Charlotte would like something to eat, she tells me no, of course, nothing to drink either. She makes her way to the kitchen doors (the ones of glass), and she looks out onto the yard, past the porch, and beyond the trees, to some faraway horizon. Her eyes look out onto the world so empty, as though there is no beauty in the branches or the wind or the sun's rays. She looks out onto nothingness for quite a while, and I, having nothing else to do, watch her watch the world. Suddenly without warning, she begins her move to the study, where she sits down upon the sofa facing the window where she could continue to watch the world. I sit across at my desk, gathering some papers and writing some statements, in between pausing to check on her.

Two hours of this has gone by, and neither of us have gone to sleep since yesterday; each of us have now been awake for twenty-four hours. I must fix myself coffee. I excuse myself, but Charlotte does not acknowledge my leaving, which is not unexpected. I fix her a plate of her favorite scones and bring her a cup of coffee as well, but it is no use. She is frozen in time, and as I look into those sad, piercing eyes, in their silence, they speak to me as if they were a cell and some lonesome voice was trapped inside. I cannot help but share the sorrow of my dear. I cannot stand the state she is in. "Charlotte, I will be going out to gather some groceries and other items, you will be staying here for a while, so I want you to become as comfortable as possible. I will try to be quick. You know I do not want to leave you, but you will have the house to yourself, all the quiet in the world. Please don't discourage from anything, the books, the kitchen, the beds, it is all yours now. Alright then, I'll be back." I finish, gently turning away from her towards the door. One foot out the door, and I hear her struggle to speak,

"William," She whispers. Instantaneously I turn to her.

"Thank you." she speaks. I nod in response, leaving her to her silence.

I know emptiness is the most comforting at times when all you feel is grief. Somehow, we managed to sit in that house for the entire morning. I haven't told her the entirety of my reason for absence. Not only would I be retrieving groceries, but I should be, not so far as the town square, but right next door retrieving her items from her room to bring home. I imagine the course of action I should take is to build her a new room. Once everything is retrieved, I will make her dinner, then draw her a bath; then at this time, I will equip the room with all of her things or however else I may find the time to do so in secrecy. I hope her reaction is not upsetting. I don't know how seeing her things from her own home in mine will settle. I had told the officer to meet me at 1:30 on her old steps. Funny. I have never stepped foot onto her porch, despite all the time she has spent on mine, and never have I seen the walls of her home; today marks the first. The sight of her room, laced at the brim with subtle tones of pink, so innocent, so bright. The brightness sparks some warm feeling in me, to which packing it all away with the officer feels much like attending a funeral for someone you didn't know all too well when they were living, but you go to support the ones you do know, alive, the ones in grief. However, as the body lies in the casket for viewing, you are stuck now staring into the lost loved one's eyes, and all you can do is remember who you are there in support of, but still, there is a void for when looking upon the dead, you wish to be sad, but you are not, and you feel as though you are the impostor as if you should only be looking through the glass, not standing within the room. To make matters more difficult, the officer cannot stop going on about how he simply can't believe what happened and how terrible he feels (the only part which I could agree with) and how he is so glad for Charlotte to have someone like me who would change his life around in an instance for her. The whole ordeal feels like an interrogation, but of course, I keep my cool entirely, telling him how it was just what I was raised to do, including a story of how my aunt taught me by taking me in to never turn down the responsibility of helping another soul. The officer could nearly shed a tear at my performance though barely any effort was put in on my part. Appealing to a southerner is not quite a task; simply mention the Lord or a common enemy, and you are golden.

I manage to make it through the rest of the packing, and he leads me out of Charlotte's home, her old home. As we pass through the parlor one last time, the officer leads the way, providing me the opportunity while his back is turned to overlook the scene. In just a second of a glance, I can feel the tense sensation of the bullet in my chest, the sound of his fingers pulling the trigger, and the sound of

Charlotte's scream. All of it. I cannot begin to empathize with my dear, but I may at least try to help her. And so, the officer locks the door and makes his way down the drive as I make mine towards my home to drop Charlotte's things in the side room, then begin again to make my way to town in search of her favorite foods, candies, chocolates, sodas, anything that may cheer her up in the slightest and at no expense should I quit.

Prior to reaching the main road, had I the slightest inclination, I would be walking into a war zone—the tension in the air as everyone stops to stare before continuing their conversations which are full of speculations about Charlotte, her family, and her situation. Then bombs away, and one by one, marketgoers flog me with their questions, concerns for her safety, rumors, and offers of services or baked goods. So, the act goes on. I answer their questions, protecting Charlotte's privacy, assuring the town of her safety, and accepting their offers, with not a single speculation as to why I, William, the new neighbor, could care for their most precious Charlotte, who I have only known a season. Thank God for the silence in that department for no one would ever understand my love. But for now, they understand my quick action toward civil responsibility and southern hospitality. One lady even tells me, "You have such a big house, you should be offering up rooms; put it to use. Awfully selfish, one man in such a big house!" The comment is well received among the crowd and even more so by myself, for I know they are on my side; they see my act as an act of kindness, my being a true gentleman. As the conversation lingers far enough along, I warn, "Well, Charlotte has been alone for a bit of time, and I want to make sure she is alright. I should truly hurry and gather my things." The mob agreeing in their condolences, allows me to pass. Although, they all mostly leave the building only to watch me from their new formation outside, beyond the glass. Off I go, through the aisles, snacks galore, chocolate by the boxes, just a few sodas to top it off, ice cream. Now, I know Charlotte won't be able to resist this. Since the ice cream melts so quick, I rarely ever buy it, so it shall make quite the nice surprise if I hurry home. And so, I do, checking out, avoiding any complex communication regarding the situation with Charlotte, just the typical, 'how are your wife's flowers doing?' 'The weather is just right today!' and so forth. As soon as he finishes, I'm off. The crowd outside disperses totally stealth and I pass on. On my trip home, I can feel their stares upon my neck, but I do not look back; no, I am far stronger than any Orpheus they would expect of me, only forward. Though do I cheat them of their retrieval of my soul for I am only looking towards my awaiting darling?

There she sits in her endless despair, gazing wondrously and sorrowfully out upon the yard that once belonged to her, a place so close, now, which feels so far, taunting her in its distance.

"Charlotte, I bought you some things, your favorite of things." Minutes pass, she shows no sign of care. "Charlotte, please, I know you are in pain; I know you have been through the unimaginable, and your mind is in a place I cannot begin to know, but you cannot lose yourself to the misery. My dear, I can't help but see you this way. Please, Charlotte, tell me what it is I can do for you?"

Her eyes climb from the floor, up to the window, and her collarbone rises and falls with her breath, "A walk." she speaks! Immediately turning her gaze to me.

"Then we shall go for one."

I walk into the kitchen, throw down my things, and place the ice cream into the freezer, quickly making my way back to her, slightly lifting her off of the couch, and supporting her along on our way out of the door. I pull her close to the right side of me, blocking her view of her home as best as I can, talking on about the wondrous willows, the breath of the air, the feeling of doing so nearly guilting as if I am dragging her lifelessly along all the while parading in the day's glories. The entirety of the situation is all just a confusing and profound feeling, the joy I have found in what has caused Charlotte so much pain. We come to the end of the driveway turning right, wandering just to the outskirts of Main Street, making another right down the woodsy path, the route we once took that seems so long ago, the route to church, except Charlotte is not planning on going near the church. I blindly follow her as she cuts between trees and ducks below branches. Finally, we reach her supposed destination, the lake. She stands silently, facing the water just as I do the same, believing it is what she wants from me until, almost bizarrely, she begins to rip off her clothes, violently unbuttoning her dress, forcing off her socks, and throwing her shoes onto the ground, in the next moment diving into the water.

"Charlotte!" I gasp.

She surfaces to tell me, "I just felt like I wanted to go somewhere."

I begin to undress, pulling off my shirt, undoing my belt, my pants falling to the ground, and my shoes removed. I, too, follow in pursuit, diving into the depths of our own despair. Upon surfacing the water, I couldn't help but be met by the most gorgeous girl, one with beauty so divine you could mistake her for a fallen angel with her skin glowing in the sun's rays, the water reflecting the light causing her not only to glow but dazzle as she moves. She looks to me, immediately breaking out into a feeble laughter, full of more of a sigh than of joy, but still laughter.

"You didn't have to jump in!" she exclaims, nearly in guilt.

"I had to! Something just came over me." I explain in return.

"I didn't realize the feeling of jumping into the unknown was mutual." she remarks.

My dearest reader, I wish you could imagine so vividly the ineffable beauty of the scene; our two bodies dancing beneath the water, below the willows, breathing in the southern air, the two of us, touched by the sun, nearly naked beneath our Lord. The closest account of its beauty could only possibly be that of the garden of Eden, the forbidden act providing for all the more enchantment. Underwater, her body grabs onto mine. For me to feel her skin against my own is a dream fulfilled, her hair falling upon my shoulders, her arms wrapped around my body with a grip affirming that I am hers and she is mine.

We had spent an hour or two more like this beneath the blissful wind until finally, hunger besieged her, and we returned home to eat. By the time she could muster the strength to finish a single meal, it was dark, and once more, she asked to go for a walk, and so, we went. Some people, when suffering from trauma eat, some go to church, some go to a therapist; for Charlotte, she walks; a way for her to face the very town her family once lived about, to breathe the very air, the coping strategy much different from running. No, she is not walking to escape but to face the day, and the memories of all that once was, each step pacifying a strangling anxiety. Being our second walk today, she has made many great strides towards resuscitation. We enter our home now as it is nearly entirely pitch black, and we both having not slept much within the past few days retreat upstairs, where Charlotte is met with her surprise. The sly project in which I have been in attempt to take forth; a painted room, soft white, with airy curtains, her trunks of clothes, photos across her walls, and with new books for her shelves, she turns to me,

"You did this. Wow. I— thank you!"

I only give as much as a smile in return. I figure at the least, having a room that feels as though it is already your own is better than returning to a bleak hole of which you should only find yourself reminded of the life you have lost, the one you must pack up and bear new to.

I let her change, as do I; the evening, discrete, I walk to her room to wish her goodnight, to turn her in and wish her soundness sleep, kissing her forehead, she lays ghostly, lost in a vast world. I exit, lengthening my stride, shutting off her light, and I leave her. Just twenty feet away, I must succumb to the great fantasies that await within my slumber as I lie in bed, rekindling the flame of what was today in the pond. At some point, my thoughts turn to dreams, and maybe just a few hours of sleep have passed, but a terrible wailing has awoken me now. At first, startled, I was confused at what the noise exactly was until I heard the deep exhales and sniffs, continuing the cycle of wails and coughs. My dearest, poorest Charlotte, how I can't stand to hear her pain. Amongst her cries, an interruption surfaces, a creak of the door. Her footsteps echo in the halls until they meet their destination, and I feel her outside my door. It isn't much longer until the door, like her own, just moments ago, begins to creak forward.

"I don't think I can be alone." she tells me, working to hold back her tears to her best ability.

"Come here," I ask of her. And so, she does. I pull the covers open enough for her to position herself beside me. She lays, her face towards mine just two, maybe three inches away,

"I'm just so scared all of the time." she confides in me.

"You are safe here Charlotte," I warn.

"For some reason, I believe you. Of course, I shouldn't believe anyone, but I believe you."

This is all she says until she turns her head away from mine, angling her body into my own. I wrap my arms around her, and just as I do, the composure she mustered was lost and had broken loose once again. All the tears she carried locked inside fall into streams, and harder she cries than before. You see, it is in the night when the grief hits, and it is in the night when she has no other to turn to. I am her only hope, the only one to hold her in her wails of inescapable pain. It is for this reason I have her all to my own; for this selfish, immoral reason, I should have the love of my lifetime in my hands in all hours of the night. And so, I whisper, holding her still, my arms tight around her thin waist, "Goodnight, Charlotte." She shudders but calms her tears.

34

The preceding week had been bleak, each day resembling the one just before; every day she spent in bed, or if she had the strength, she took on the walk from her room to the study, though, in either room, she stared endlessly out the window. I was forced to leave her sometimes each day for work or food, but all other hours were spent sitting by her, with her, watching her. In the wake of the terror of that night, she had no composure; upon moving in, the depression only set foot. It's a horrible thing watching someone suffer a million battles when you cannot pick up a sword. What is there to do but let time heal what cannot be touched but what lies deep within? Only a month remains, about a month, thirty-four days until civil duty calls. I have worked in the office much more frequently, which is not to my liking since it pains me to leave Charlotte, but I am planning another trip. One for more than a day, for Charlotte and me to spend the rest or almost the rest of the summer somewhere far from the reminders of her horror. Charlotte, like myself, when faced with situations that prove greater than we can manage, flee, it may be argued this method is ineffective, I say non-abrasive. I have been planning a trip to the North; we will trek upward to New York for her to experience a world unknown to her, one parallel to her home. I will take her to libraries, films, the theater, and shops. What have we here anyway? And when we return, we return, but we return with adventure. It seems I have curated the perfect plan; a plan I shall present to Charlotte tomorrow evening after I have made my final return home from the office. How magnificent it shall be to see the streetlights waver in her eyes, the blue hue contrasting her skin, her smile at the sight of the Empire State Building. Some final touches and then the plan shall be presented tomorrow, just around the corner. At this moment, I find myself in the center of the street, retreating from the law office. I suppose it is myself who put me into this position; if only I hadn't peeked in, hadn't made myself known, then I wouldn't have so many obligations so soon. If only I waited, followed the words of ink seated onto my contract. But there is no need for me to grieve lost time when establishing myself as a trusted public servant has entrusted my image into all of the hearts of the souls within this town. Regardless, I am home now, on my front steps, the sacred steps, where I know, I shall not return to the office until my true starting date. I bid everyone a-do, a goodbye, an hasta la vista, if you will. The doors I face now, the time continuum that swings open to restart the summer clock and, with a creak, "Charlotte, I am home."

"Oh, hello, hello!" Charlotte exclaims with a tone one may mistake for cheer.

"Hello, Charlotte, where are you? You aren't in the study?" I ponder and return in a much more questioning tone as I have barely heard her speak above a whisper.

"Well... I'm in the kitchen; come find me!" she cheers once more. And so, I do, to find her in the kitchen where she stands over a bowl mixing away, so it would seem.

"Why, Charlotte, you are up! You are cooking?" I remark with a tone full of question yet astonishment.

"Oh yes, I'm up. Come on, I'm not lame now, am I?" she jokes as if forgetting the last weeks. In my scattered train of thought, she begins to hum, to hum!

"Charlotte, please tell me, what has changed so soon, so fast? Your heart, it seems your heart beats again, a different speed, and the color to your face it had returned; your eyes now are only as blue as they once were, not overcast by a sorrowful kind."

"You talk in such riddles, you know. Nothing about me deserves this, really. So, preserve your remarks; I'm just the same."

"No, Charlotte, you must recognize you have returned to normal." I pull her hands from the bowl, assisting her in cleansing them, then walking her to the kitchen table, yes, you know, the one by the glass doors. I hold her hands as we sit eye to eye, and I ask doing my best to look past her façade, "Charlotte, what has brought you home?"

"Ok, ok. Well, earlier, about a couple of hours ago, some of my old school friends came by, Marcy and Jane, I hope it's ok, but I let them in, and they told me I looked horrible, but this wasn't what pulled me back to life. You see, we talked of superfluous things for a few moments about the summer, their trips, new dresses, you know and all of a sudden, Marcy asks if you were my new dad. The girl never has known how to keep her mouth shut, but it was when she said this that I realized..."

I attempt desperately to not express the urgency inside of me, the quickening of my heartbeat as I have been referred to as my dear's new father when I wish nothing but the opposite for us. I hold myself back and listen only tentatively as she continues,

"Well, I realized I may not know exactly what a father should do for his daughter, how he should behave, or what he should say, but I know that the love I feel for you outcast that which I felt for him by an eternity. Our love, you and I's is more than the fatherly kind. This realization made me so repulsed by the girl I told her quite sternly, and I believe loudly that you are not my father, to this I believe ole Marcy took it that I was upset. I don't believe she could uncover the complexity of my emotions, so they did all they could, smiled and nodded as they waved goodbye out the door."

As Charlotte finished her story, I could only pray she couldn't see the visible signs of my gratitude for her emotions towards me, her acclaiming of our love which she, too, believes to be so divine. "Oh, my dear, I hope you know how glad I am to see you this way!" I sing. I didn't know what else to say without completely giving myself away to her.

"Back to that, so you see, it was this realization that led me here. I finally understood that I was weeping over a man and his actions, a man and a woman wed in complete contemptibility neither able to fulfill their duties as parents. Though I was locked in grief for my mother, who deserved nothing of what she got, I was locked in the state by him; even when I live miles away with him behind bars, and with me free, surrounded in love, still, he locks me behind bars with him, behind iron engraved with his name. I cannot let him win. I can't let him, not when I have you. He cannot keep me away from you when I have you so near. So, I got up, I started cooking, and no longer will I allow myself to be chained to the sorrows of the past when all of my hope sits inches away holding my hands."

To this confession, this manifestation of love, could I keep my lips sealed as they part consistently attempting to warp into a smile. Oh, how I wish only to yell out, 'I love you, Charlotte! I love you, I do!' But I know these three words should damn me, and so whether by Lucifer or the Lord someone had held my tongue down as all I can now say in return is, "And you believe I am the one to speak in riddles."

She laughs as she can sense we both have much more we wish to say but know would be better kept within, for if we were to say what was on our hearts, we would have to face reality, a reality that makes truth the most difficult fruit to bare.

In this moment, it is quite difficult to withhold my plans for our trip, and with the exhilaration of her return to me, I have no choice but to share my ideas. "Charlotte, why don't we leave here?" I expel. Although, I believe there may have been better phrasing, for she only looks at me with confusion.

"Leave... here? Your home? Why and to where?" she asks concerningly.

"Well, I thought we could go up to the coast, all the way north to New York," I explain.

"For how long?" she questions, seeming overtaken by the idea.

"Just for a few weeks."

"A few weeks!"

I know now that the idea was obscure, for she has no apprehension to join me on said trip. "You don't want to take a trip, to get out of the country for a while, see what lies beyond Georgia?" I ask her.

"No, no, no, I want to stay. I want to be here with you in the country, in Georgia. I can't leave now. I would only feel like I am running away from my burdens when I know I would only return to the grief once more. If none of this had happened, I would have jumped at the idea, but I know now that I only wanted to run away from what lay within the walls of my home and now, I do not have those worries anymore. I can enjoy the air and the rivers with you and my favorite of the seasons without the fear of what watched us from my windows. If we left now, we would miss out on what there is for us here."

"Charlotte, I understand. I thought a trip might help, but I understand now the idea was foolish; frankly, I am proud of you for rejecting. I know finishing the summer here without a dreadful watch will be utterly splendid and so I ask you to forget the idea entirely. We shall certainly stay and enjoy the beauty granted to us that surrounds us already."

"Thank you, William."

Although the idea of a trip to the coast was thrilling at the thought—taking Charlotte far away from what she knew, leaving her only to me in a car, in a hotel, or a theater—she was right in wanting to stay. In losing her family, the clouds no longer linger above us, casting a dreadful frown, but the clouds have opened to allow the sun to shine through like inseparable beams, casting the image of the heavens above our divine affair. She is, as always, entirely right. And so, we go on, her as happy as ever, and I entirely complete.

"What shall it be, a trip to the pond, to the Willow?" she asks me to choose.

"Why not go to our tree? I can pack us some food."

"Sounds marvelous! Why not bring some books along too?"

35

My patient audience, I hope you will not be fooled as our story does not end in our rekindling, yet only begins again. And so, just as it used to be, the minutes turned into hours and the days into weeks; as each moment passed, we float further into an endless abyss of irrevocable bliss, a never-ending solitude in which I find my home in her, and she gains one in me. This day, a Saturday, we awoke to the sounds of the birds outside our windows, to the smell of the dew left by the rain on the grass, and to the sound of the willow's branches tapping at our door, awaiting us to begin our dance through our home and out into the nature that awaits. Before Charlotte, back in Maine, I had never found myself outdoors frequently. I had sat at the docks with my aunt though I never even had thought to put my feet in; I stayed fully clothed at all times, buttoned up with a belt and loafers. Alas, look at me now as she undresses me with each glance; I stay at a moment's notice, completely willing to unclothe myself for the lake, for the heat. Every day is an astonishment. Regardless of the activity, often we mimic just the day before, with nothing much to do in the countryside, with no one more to meet or to find the company. Though this is what affirms the divinity of our own relations, that in consistent repetition, not one day is the same, and not a conversation is relapsed. She is the personification of the definition of indescribable, from her beauty to her laugh, her interests, to the very feeling she invokes. I pity my reader, for you may never understand. I often laugh at the man I used to be as I believed I had lived; I know now how wrong I was as I have lived more in a season than in the decades that have amassed me. A bewilderment she is. Before my plunge into the pieces of my heart, I said each day was much like the one before with inactivity, and so just the same; on this Saturday, Charlotte awakes quite slowly. At least, slowly as in, it is nearly nine o'clock, 8:47 am to be precise. She believes me a fool in this matter as she says she does not wake late; it is I who is simply too early and apparently too early for my own good. Regardless, I tell her I am just overly excited to see her that I cannot sleep. This, she perceives as a comedic lie, a bit of sarcasm, though to me, it is not one bit off from the truth. Of course, she would think me a fool if I truly told her I could no longer sleep peacefully in my own home as a result of her heavenly body just down my hall. It is only on the occasion that when she is sad, she makes the walk down the hall and into my room, where she finds welcoming her with open arms. Still, I find myself in joy as she finds herself in despair. Again, I find myself losing my very train of thought in the thought of her. As in my distraction, she appears from down the steps; she travels so light, I never hear her arrival. It is only until I see her face that I know she awaits me to begin her day. This day, Saturday, (as I hope you would remember) we shall go to town. An act which Charlotte despises, however one that must be done. How she so flatteringly chooses to accompany me despite her hatred, she tells me that going to town was her favorite thing to do when she was younger, that she lived obviously not far from Main Street, but she was locked to the outskirts where her home resides and could only so often make the trip when accompanied by a family member or a group of friends. She said the trip was only ever reserved for weekends. She loved it as it gave her a glimpse of life in the city. As she walked into town, she could imagine she was walking onto the streets of New York City; she loved the ice cream bar and climbing up on the counter to place her order, she enjoyed talking to each of the inhabitants of the place. Yet today, the once beloved activity is one of her most dreaded. I believe from how she speaks of it that she can't stand the people; how they look at her as a lost dog in the pound, what her old friends may think of her, how they must regret ever once stepping foot into her old home, each of the inhabitants who pity her yet feel disgusted at ever once communicating with her father. She never once associated herself with him yet now she pays for his wickedness. He continues to outstretch his hell upon her even when she is beyond his reach. I believe this very twisted fact is an unavoidable product of trauma as when I was younger, Charlotte's age, so to think, I shuddered at my own voice, the very accent which possessed me as if trying to hear the voice of my father. It was a curse. No matter the length I traveled to separate myself from him and my mother, no matter the sanction I found in my aunt, they were with me each time I decided to open my mouth. In time, I so gratefully grew out of this or grew into the pain as now I am glad for the remnants of my accent as it reminds me of my childhood home and of my aunt who similarly after living in America for so long intertwined both accents to create a loose version of the one she had before.

My tangent has taken just enough time for Charlotte to finish her breakfast and for her to seek my attention, for us to make our way. We depart, making our way down that oh-so-familiar drive, once so long, now a collection of our memories, our story weaved between the trees. Today we have left a bit early, just enough so that as we turn the corner and civilization awaits, staring us down, we are not met with each and every townsperson completely yet, as some may still be asleep, others eating, the men at work, women in the yards bringing in the night's laundry and so the majority (I may say) are occupied to some degree. Sunday, though, as today is Saturday, is a situation that mirrors only the polarity of today. Sunday is the day when every last inhabitant, with no exception, flocks to the church for morning worship, often which lasts until noon, but it does not end there, no, no then there is the luncheon which follows, lasting until three (on a good day), then in following, the men may flock to one another to discuss their newest tool set or the news in a fragmented, small-

minded sense of course. The women then go on to attend
to the children reading, singing, or playing with them all
in the small field, situated beside the church. Often, I find
myself begrudgingly inside that very church, situated in a
pew, nearly every Sunday. You could say to maintain
appearances, to be the good neighbor, or a Christian man,
the woman, they swoon, the men invite me in on their
conversations; to attend church is to be one of them, to
not, is to be of a heretic or sort. It's hard to say what is
within the southerner's mind when beneath the peachy
grin is a silent judgment, and this was not a hard fact to
learn. I would not fear judgment if it weren't for Charlotte
to hide what seems to encompass my whole world in plain
sight, the part I play in the charade the town endures day
after day, yet no one has yet to realize they are all simply
jesters within my court for I have crafted the most
beautiful sonnet to which we dance and parade day upon
day, providing a reason for my recent absence in church.
Yes, you see, Charlotte like myself, is not a church going
person. Just another trait we share, I should say she was
but for reasons far from holy, a simple means of escape it
was to her, so today in the past weeks we have been able
to deter speculation through my dear's grand
performances—her monologues on the amount of pain
her heart has had to bear, that, for now, religion plays no
stakeholder when she cannot bear the light of day. She
goes on and on each day. I believe she hopes that she may
have my approval to continue the charade into the school
year. She loves education and reads just as any young
scholar may, but she cannot take the aggravation of her

peers, even of her teachers. She wants more of life, yet she only wants to maintain so little; a sophistic girl with a scope of illusions which, if all unraveled, should circle the world three times around. Though this particular display of hers casts a shadow of gloom large enough it could cover us all, the town, of course, finds it best to leave the sad young girl to me, who they believe can somehow manage it all, they don't realize how easy it is when it is love, but that's the point. Charlotte and I lead flawless performances never even discussed between her and me; only naturally have they taken course. We float down that main road which she fills with shadows as the members of the town still cannot resist their stares; the idea of what event took place in her life, in her young life, remains unfathomable. This is only another solidifying factor in our love for one another; only she and I can see the beauty within the horror. Each time Charlotte stumbles into town with me, the sympathy meets no end. Her schoolmates who would once flaunt around the town without a single care for Charlotte, the ones who once would sit in the ice cream parlor each night without even a slight turn of the head if Charlotte's name were to be called. These very girls who insist on calling themselves friends of Charlotte now rush up to her at first sight (if not preoccupied, of course); the ones in discussions with young boys of their age, and in particular muscular pristine may not dare to part ways from their delinquent converseness. However, the ones untested at the moment of Charlotte's arrival nearly trip over one another's bodies to greet her with each unsufferable ballot they can think up, 'How are you handling it?' 'How can you live with such pain?' 'It must have been so horrible! I just couldn't imagine!' Most often, each line she is greeted with is phrased as a question, a question which would mean each end of each phrase is plastered with a question mark, you know, the squiggle which determines to a reader such as you or me that something is being asked. This knowledge is not unbeknownst to the common man, yet for each question of how Charlotte could manage or of how she feels, lies no search for an answer. Charlotte understands this. All they expect in return is her silence for it is all they can take. A lack of compassion one may ask, or of common sense, may another. All I hear when each "friend" appraises my dear with a question is simply another bullet— a bullet of artificiality. Before you may wish to contradict my words, I am not unfamiliar with the rhetorical question. I simply believe for one to care means to ask with meaning and not with weightless, attention-consuming intention. Perhaps I am a bit hard on the girls, on the other townspeople who follow similar suits, or perhaps I am too deeply in love.

Upon managing to break away from the self-absorbed entourage, we make our way to the store we know so well. We may never find falsity in the storekeeper's grin, the main mart, where my first acquaintance, the most awkward man, still remains, completely incognizant of Charlotte's livelihood. A selfishness which takes the form of a man in a way unrelated to the one previously witnessed, one which disguises itself as a mere disconnection to one's surroundings, though indeed a means of ignoring everyone except oneself. It appears no matter how hard we try selfishness is rooted in us all. Charlotte enjoys the store the most for said man and for his complete lack of care for her. She may prance around, doing whatever she may wish, and he will remain unknowing, uninterrupted from his own thoughts, that is, until she may buy something, which at this point, we do, and we evoke irritation immediately as we place our items down in front of him. He does not speak until minutes pass of checking out our items, he feels compelled to fill the silence, "The shipment of milk came late." Just like that, he spoke, yet that was all there was to say. My Charlotte decided to reply, "Oh no, should we be careful drinking it. How late exactly was it?" Not in worries for the expiration, but to see the look on his face as he realizes that he may have lost a coin in telling his own troubles. Nonetheless, we proceed to buy the milk, and with only silence for the remainder of the purchase, we find ourselves on our way with only a few moments more. Though Charlotte had been bombarded already by the majority of those her doom seems to attract, it does not surprise, as in our attempt to flee, she is greeted continuously along the way. While treading towards the road which will take us home, she asks if I would like to stop by my office, a kind offer, I suppose, but I neglect immediately as she knew I had made my word and that I should not return until my originally intended start date. It is now that I realize in her recession, she had little faith I intended to keep my promise. We nearly made our way to our hidden path beyond the church and through the woods, but we decided collectively we should not in order to get the groceries home safe and the milk to a refrigerator. Though, I am sure we will make our way in a similar direction, if not today, tomorrow, for a day on the lake. She had pressed on about getting back into the water; frankly, I find it as a surprise myself that I had not allowed for it sooner.

Planting ourselves home in the kitchen, we sort the food, placing each item in its designated location. In finishing, Charlotte does not make her way to the kitchen table or the study but to the grand room beyond the kitchen, the room which I have barely set foot into in my own home. I, still in the kitchen, hear through the hall, "William, come in here, quick!"

Without a second thought, I launch to her side, "Charlotte, what is it that could cause such a scare?"

"This room!" she exclaims as if not already unbeknownst to me as I stand behind her in the very room that casts such supposed terror. "Well, it's a disaster to say it simply," she continues.

"Charlotte, I do not think it looks so bad. What do you find so preposterous?"

"You haven't touched it since you moved in. Look, paintings and gold frames you have just stacked upon one another awaiting their hanging, wallpaper half-peeled from the wall, dust galore, should I continue?"

"No, no, I see it as quite clear." With a moment to take it in, "What do you suppose we do?"

She jolts at the question as if she had prepared plans of interior decoration for centuries, "Well, I say strip the wallpaper, paint it white, hang the portraits, move one of the couches from this side of the room to a more central location. You'll need a small table of some sort, clean the rug definitely, then dust, dust again. Maybe some new lights. Oh, a chandelier! You could have balls in here if you so wished!"

With such overwhelming excitement, it appears in just a moment, Charlotte has transformed into a decorator. I interrupt, "Charlotte, Charlotte, we can do whatever it is you wish to this room, whatever you dream, and I will create it but when shall we begin it all, now, so soon, we will have to go to town again."

"No, I suppose we don't need to do it all now, but we can start peeling the paper and dust at least."

I had no inclination this project would have been taken on with such an urge just minutes prior, but I suppose I do seem to have neglected this portion of the home, a large portion that has gone completely unused. I am not opponent to more work. Never in my life had I ever gotten my hands so covered in paint before Georgia. Why not allow the craftsmanship to continue? Before I could blink, she had already begun tearing the seams of paper from the walls, throwing each onto the ground behind her.

"Quick, grab me a chair to stand on!" She demands.

I rush to grab a chair from the side of the kitchen table. Look at me, fetching chairs at the immediate call of a girl peeling wallpaper methodically from a room we have rarely stepped foot into. What a thought, one that had called for an immediate repugnance without even having to flee my mind.

"Well, are you going to start peeling?"

I can only laugh at my willingness to comply, as one does if one were a dog, I presume. I go to the nearest wall to peel the paper and throw it behind me just as she. It is only now on the third piece that I realize why she must find such joy in the act. How I find you can take out all of your aggression through paper. I assume this was her internal reality calling, her means of intentional destruction to act as a treatment for her pain. We both pull and throw and pull and throw. She moves closer to me to tear a piece; this time, not so manically, rather quite carefully, she rips, caring to its end; with the final pull, she chants, "I bet you can't rip off a piece longer than mine!"

A game was what her act of unintended care was intended to begin, I take her challenge. Pulling just as she, working slowly, soothing the piece with my hand as I move simultaneously up the wall. My last bit, and I hold it beside her own,

"No. Mine is larger." she protests.

"I believe it is quite clear, Charlotte, that it is not the largest."

"Well, I believe it is," she contests.

"Then I shall simply allow you to believe it."

She lets out a most playful grunt and lunges at me as if to begin a fight. I lift her off for her to return to me with soft grabs and pushes. She locks her leg around my own, and in an instance, we fall onto the floor, the floor covered high in wallpaper. Upon meeting the ground, Charlotte lets out a large laugh; her most angelic laughter would have anyone join in laughter even when not finding themselves next to her fallen upon the floor. Continuing our match in a flood of laughter cushioned by paper, she climbs upon me, her legs straddling my torso; as she lifts her hands nearly above her head, she threatens a foe punch. I grab her legs, with each one of my hands around her calves, nearly making their way all the way around, one index finger runs its way down to her ankle, while my other hand finds its way up to her thigh. May I control its path before it may climb higher? She shows not a sign of bother, not a sign of care, as if my hands around her are just of second nature. My body, I hope shows no sign of care to her as I feel the tingle that lingers as she rocks herself forward. Her hands remain high; she has yet to follow through, and in what is a moment to her is an eternity to me as she plays with much more than her fists. Finally, she relieves me of my lock, rolling over to lay back by my side. She laughs unstably. The two of us, now, lay staring up at the ceiling.

"We should paint the ceilings just like Michelangelo, with clouds, and angels, and people of high morality," Charlotte explains.

"Do you know how to paint?" I inquire.

"No, do you?"

"No, I do not."

"Oh well, rather we can imagine the ceilings painted like Michelangelo's work. Close your eyes, and you will see it."

I obey, locking my eyes to feel hers looking to mine, her eyes searching my body for her to recognize the quickness of my breath, the sensation deep within me. Finally, I open my eyes and turn to her as she lays upon my side, with her face at mine, her eyes fixated on my own as I fight the greatest battle within myself. One of temptation versus resistance.

"Did you see it?" she whispers.

"Yes. And... I see an ant."

She lets out just about a scream, "Where! Where is it?"

As I wanted to lay by her side, staring at the ceiling into eternity with one another, there was a separate scenario painting itself upon the ceiling, which did not resemble one of Michelangelo's works but one of my own provocative creations. This, you see, is a sacrifice I am forced to make each day for the protection of my young Charlotte's decency,

"It must have come from all the dusty paper," she rationalizes.

"Presumably," I contend.

"Why don't we call it a day in here?" she asserts.

"Sounds good to me." She laughs, leading me out of the room, past the kitchen, and onto the porch where we sit to watch the sunset, her head falling with the sun onto my shoulder, my hand pulling hers into mine.

36

It seems so soon that the sky falls just to rise again. We come, awakened to another day, yet again. It's often that I wonder what more there is to say. Still, in the mundane life, I live there with Charlotte, who, when intermixed with mundanity, ignites curiosity, bringing dimension to my previously one-dimensional world. A change that can be mentioned for today as it hasn't nearly begun, is that I hear Charlotte in the bathroom already; yes, she rose before me. This, I tell you is a rarity. Soon after, a small knock. With the creak of my door and for a morning that has only lasted a mere ten minutes, I see the sunshine again as Charlotte's face peers between the gap of the door. Checking to see if I was awake to which, of course, she finds me with my eyes open.

"Darn! I thought for once I beat you!"

"And you did beat me up in technicality."

"I guess so, but you are awake now too."

"Is that so much of a disappointment?" I ask inquiringly.

"No!"

From there, she begins slamming the door, she has just slid herself in between, jolting onto my bed, nearly on top of me. Her force so triumphant, she shakes the frame as she topples upon me.

"Well, good morning, Charlotte."

"Well, good morning, William."

She attempts to mimic me while exaggerating my accent, of course. I take it that this action was her silent exposition of the fact she was not disappointed in finding me awake. I realize at this moment, as Charlotte is so close that I can feel her breath on my lips, that I have found myself with her divine body upon me. It is no longer that I can keep all of my behavior under control with her the reaffirming goddess who places herself upon me. Just as Hera would Zeus, this would be a test from the gods. I fail as I pull my hand from my side, hidden below the blanket, reaching to her hip and running it up her skin, my eyes unmoving from her own. My hand reaches her back, where it remains only momentarily before retreating to find her chin. To hold her face in my hand is to hold my very own angel not just in my arms for once but to have her very face in my hand, controlling her jaw, maintaining her eyes' reflection in mine. Still, she says not one word as we both remain in silence, only the room chimes a thousand words which must all be left unsaid. Our eyes each one's own. We are locked in a love that grapples with no kind of love known to man, neither that of a father, of a friend, nor a significant other. I am prohibited by the secret code I have yet to break. What shall we call the love of Charlotte and William? What can we call it at all? For this, I run my hand down from her cheek onto her neck only to grab a lock of hair which I grace as my hand falls from her warmth entirely. The silence still remains, that is, until,

"We haven't been for a ride in the car in quite a long time," Charlotte informs me.

"Shall we go for a ride today?"

"Can we? That would be grand! We could go down to the lake."

"It is a bit of a grassy road, so we could go a bit of the way."

"Anything is good, or just down the road, not to town, the opposite direction through the country and back and then to the lake."

"The day is ours, but what about the grand room? When shall that project be completed?"

"Let's take a gap day, shall we?"

"As long as the gap is not so long. You don't want any more ants to escape from that paper still remaining on the floor."

"Oh, don't remind me! We will do it tomorrow or this evening. For now, you should get up and join me so we can get in the car."

Immediately following her request, she climbs to her knees in an attempt to roll my body off the bed. Upon failure, climbing over me to a stature where she attempts again to pull me down and onto the ground. I comply, getting out of bed dramatically as she wished for to get dressed for a drive.

"Perfect! I will be in the kitchen."

Before I may even ask her not to leave, she is off, darting down the stairs to her destination found on the floor below. I work swiftly to get myself situated for the day, to not disappoint, and for her not to be alone so long without my company. Finding my way to her shortly after, she sits at the kitchen table waiting, rocking her legs back and forth beneath her. She urgently awaits the ride. A ride that despite only emerging today as an idea for activity is one that has not been done in quite a while; therefore, it is for this reason that the level of excitement impedes a young girl who must await her driver.

"Finally!" she exclaims as she strides towards me, immediately flinging the keys from my hand and continuing her race out the door.

Without any room for the overactivity of questioning, it is quite clear I am to follow, for she would only be awaiting once more, not so patiently, in the passenger seat. Yes, just as expected. I only have to go as far as the porch to see my vision come true without even having on her shoes, she lies reclined in her passenger seat, feet out the window, and I, the man to fill the seat beside her, to drive her down her endless road as her hair waves in the wind, her hands sliding alongside the air out past the window. And as we go on, we take with us our safety in each other's solitude as we move through the countryside which we call home, the one which Charlotte loves so dear; we drift together on a path unknown to us, surrounded by the beauty of the natural world with one another in each other's reach, we are safe. Even when moving, Charlotte is secure.

It isn't until I check my watch that I discover we have been driving back and forth on the same four roads for nearly two hours. Between shifts of endless dialogue and silence, which express complete joy in the moment alone, time had passed further than the cars on the road pointing out such a sight to Charlotte as my watch face was to me; she only laughs at how we could spend such an exorbitant amount of time in such a small car on only an accumulation of four roads, spanning only a few miles when combined. She tells me to go for one more loop, and then we should head to the lake. I express that I believe that to be a plan, and that it is what we shall do. Past the brown yard, completely treeless, with brown grass run over by a flood of even browner hay, rotted in a lack of care which the home on the plot resembles. Past the home of a friend of Charlotte's, which she describes as a relationship having taken place moons ago, only I realize her disconnect seems to begin its falter at the time of our meeting. Past a series of quaint but respectable homes each, with a little patch of a yard to roam just enough for a dog to run and meet another by the fence. Down another road, only for a short time, until we complete our loop, reaching a drive of such familiarity the one which looks out onto what seems to be nothing but grass and trees. However, as traveling closer, you may find our hidden drive, lined with trees that look deep and far. Hidden at its end is a house, a house of a certain fellow I should know quite well. Yes, a man by the name of William. This is the drive we take only to turn off to the left of the home onto the grass, forming a road of our own, just as Charlotte had asked. Only so far is there for us to go until I must stop, and we both must walk to our next destination, the lake.

I leave the car first. She follows, only to take the lead full speed towards the water. She reaches behind to encourage me to match her stride. It appears she has learned all it takes of her is her touch, and I am hers for each command she may bring upon me. We twist our way through the pines and down the dirt to reach, at last, the glistening lake, which we look to one another as if yet another secret. Charlotte had found this place as a child when she would play in the woods; since her finding it, she used this lake as one of her many escapes. The water which covered her while swimming would hide more than her body beneath its depths but her tears which she cried when finally alone; her secret safe even from nature who may watch her, as even when in tears she would not appear as though anything was of the matter for the tears blended into the waters submerging her skin. Today she shares her secret paradise with me, whose secrets may lie within the waters as well. Each time she must unclothe herself, she reveals each piece of herself to me as a piece of light that shines brighter than the doors to eternity above. Charlotte is but a heavenly body in joy, and when she plays, as she tans and as I catch her singing to herself or when she believes, I am turned away. Charlotte, she is full of fascination— never does she find a discussion at its end, but does she have another series of matter to discuss.

Her smile moves my lips to a place I had ceased to know in my prior existence. This contagion only further spreads her grip upon my heart. It's always difficult to say how long it is we spend with one another, especially on days we find ourselves meeting the water. This day has felt only as much as forty minutes, though as I check my watch again, I recognize the time has determined it has, in fact, been nearly four hours and forty minutes. I put my watch down and dive back into the water to meet Charlotte again as we both simply laugh off the matter of what time we have wasted of the day, but what is a waste when embezzled in fun? I find my hands wrapped around my darling Charlotte's form as she holds on to me beneath the water; we find ourselves interrupted by a noise, one of which any one person may quickly assure another to have been a deer or some sort of animal, perhaps a squirrel. Charlotte, as the inquisitive delight she is, decides maybe an alligator; we laugh about the possibility, that is, until the sound of movement becomes much denser. We look around ourselves, our eyes circling our surroundings until unbeknownst to me, Charlotte spots our culprit, a schoolgirl friend, hidden behind a tree.

"What are you doing out here watching us?" she shouts, immediately sending the girl into a flee as Charlotte goes on to express her utmost annoyance of girls her own age. Although I could not tell you what it is she has said, as I can only imagine how long the girl could have been standing within the woods, how much of us she had seen, what she may have seen, what she may perceive of the situation. My imagination seems to only find the scene in which the girl finds herself running out of the woods into town, grabbing any adult or child she may find to explain how Charlotte and William are alone in the lake, very closely together underneath the water. I worry only silently within myself, but it doesn't take long for Charlotte to imagine what fears could be circulating within my mind as she assures, "Don't worry about her; she's just a desperate girl who was probably only taking an innocent walk."

"Charlotte, we need to leave immediately."

"What, the lake?"

"No, the country. Yes! Get out of the water. We must go."

"William, if she did go to town to say anything about oh I don't know us alone, or in the water, or if she were to make up some story completely and people who may be dumb enough to believe her were to follow her back to the location of the event only to find the accused had fled, well, that is sure to make us look guilty when we have nothing to be guilty about. On the other hand, if we stay and she comes back with some townsman, well then, we keep our distance, swim laps, and as they love to question, we express we are just taking advantage of the nice weather, and I was in the attempt of taking my mind off of the pain of my existence!"

Believe me, I have evaluated the situation extensively, though in the end, she is right. For us to keep our innocence, we should stay, despite the fun being extorted; leaving would only be a hopeless endeavor. Charlotte, though is completely unbothered by the situation as she returned in an instance to her lake-day activities, continuing to swim and laugh in desperate attempts to bring me into the water with her. Finally, I get in once again, but only to stand on the outskirts of the wakes. I had no intention or capability of continuing the fun we were having; my peace has been entirely ruined, and for that, I should forever hate this one young girl who wished to watch us from the depths of the woods. Charlotte appears to have arrived at the understanding that I have no ability to partake in her activity, that my mind is encapsulated in the events of earlier, and that the most I may bear to withstand is to watch her enjoy, but that I could move not but an inch closer to her. With what remains of the light of day, I imagine it is not hard for her to see the fumes protruding from my ears, the result of the immediate hatred I came to possess for this girl. She attempts to calm me, telling me, "See, the time has passed by and neither she nor has anyone else made their return." Nothing would work. My mind is held hostage by a series of emotions within a range from anger to fear, leaving no room for the joy I felt only an hour earlier. Since it has been nearly an hour, Charlotte allows us to make our way home. Thankful for her understanding of the situation, once her ability to possess rational thought reappeared, she stayed only long enough for someone who may come looking for the guilty. While understanding my position, she accompanies me in my retreat now that the time has passed.

Back we go, to our home, where we have the capability to hide within my walls, protected from the forsaken gaze of reality. The evening had come, and after dinner, the one of which I could barely eat, Charlotte found me in the study, at my desk in an attempt to read, in failure as my eyes could only look up past the window, holding their gaze, awaiting a mob, searching for the torches beyond the willows. It isn't that I may remove my gaze until I feel a hand, a soft hand, which I know so well, that of Charlotte's which she places around the back of my neck, "I'm sorry, William, for what happened, I know people can make up stories about situations like ours and you have a reputation to protect, but we have never once traveled into a place where we could find ourselves in the wrong. You have to let your fear go."

Another attempt at saving me from my own reservations. Charlotte realizes quickly her words continue to only brace the exterior of my mentality, for she decides to wrap her leg over my own to situate herself right on top of me as I continue only to sit in my chair. She looks at me now blankly in the eyes as mine try to wander away to the window, a place one's eyes would never dare to set foot with Charlotte so close. Her one hand lies still behind my neck while the other pulls my face away from the glass towards her eyes once more. We find ourselves in a familiar place, lost in each other's eyes. Her thumb traces my cheek back and forth; in the silence with her in my arms, I find peace. She recognizes her power; she moves her face in closer proximity to my own for her lips to take residence not but an inch away from my own, for her to whisper, "If you would like, I can do something that should indeed incite a worry."

I cannot but sigh as she, I find is the one possessor of my body, the keeper of my soul. She has whittled her way into my bloodstream, releasing an ecstasy that travels within me at the speed I find my heart travels now; she moves into me further only to hold me above the cliffs, close enough she travels, to then drop me off as she moves simply to kiss my cheek.

"Another time." she whispers so gallantly.

Though she does not remove her body from mine. She remains on my lap, reading a book in her same position, distressing my nerves. I wonder how it may feel for a young girl to know she encompasses the heart, body, and mind of a man? 'Another time' she tells me. When, my Charlotte? In a time more hopeless perhaps? More forsaken? I wonder what time we may find ourselves more faceted in a mixture of joy and pain than this, for what time may she await? I know the time now; it is the time that this day, one which spiraled to a place unimaginable, may come to an end, and we may see each other in tomorrow's wake.

37

A morning appearing just as any other could not but feel as strange to me. Having been accompanied by the wildest array of sensations just yesterday, a day wielded upon strange circumstances, one particularly which finds its way into my most joyous dream and the other, my nightmares. Yesterday, we managed to arrive to today unscathed, but the feeling of concern has not yet fled. Just as before, Charlotte cannot stop her attempts to calm me, to persuade me of my innocence, and yet I feel the very eyes which we captured in the woods on our backs, even within my home, behind the safety of our walls. This girl has now corrupted my very well-being in my own home. Charlotte, though, remains unfazed; she has moved on from the instance. So, I try cooking her breakfast; she tells me we should get back to work, and frankly, for me and my nerves' sake, I agree. We begin quickly without a second thought, removing all of the debris to the trash bin outdoors. Now onto the laying of a cloth which I still maintain from my initial renovations, in order for us to retrieve the paint which should then be used to coat the walls of this room. I believe it should be white, though we must go to town to retrieve the paint as I do not have nearly enough here. I presume an innocent appearance should be a good thing for our public image, and we may learn whether or not we have been disgraced or when it is we should be flogged. We brace ourselves as we slowly enter the town. I, anticipating a thunder of scrutiny; Charlotte, expecting none but the usual bolstering crowd. At first sight of other town members, I nearly wince as they appear to walk towards us.

"Charlotte, how are you doing? I'm so glad you are out and about." That's all they have to say.

"I'm doing much better actually. William is even letting me redo one of his rooms in his house, you know, peeling wallpaper, painting and all. It is quite fun!" she explains in return.

I still but cannot await the return of commentary which may wish to see me hanged. But alas, the couple returns, "William, the town cannot get over just how kind of a man you are! We are just so glad to have you here." Maybe the girl didn't tell them. Perhaps they hadn't yet heard!

"No, no. I am lucky to have you all. I have never lived in a town so close and kind with one another." Yes, there you are, William, the respectable, town-seeking man you are! Employ the skills of acting to which you have become so accustomed to.

"Well, you all have a wonderful time painting." Finally, they leave us.

Immediately Charlotte looks to me, "You see."

I know just as to what she wishes to refer. Without further commentary, although we hadn't but graced the outskirts of Main Street, there lies still a whole town of possibility that stands just beyond the invisible wall where we remain. She continues on, as do I. We set immediately for the hardware to retrieve our paint canisters. Along the way, we stop for a few more check-ins with some neighbors, then again when entering the store, and a few more times within the aisles. Our final stop being the checkout counter, where the couple, who I found my first town friends in, remain day by day. We talk with one another more cheerfully and fervently than the material conversations which stand in its precedence. We catch up just as one could believe old friends would, then we depart to begin our project. Stop. Stop again. Gratefully, the weight of the paint cans provides for a wonderful means of escape. So again, we are off to take passage through that invisible wall to which I may finally feel sanctioned again in our lives, as not a single soul had any inclination of a relationship being more than anyone may innocently believe. Charlotte remains a victim of domestic brutality, and I, the grand savior. Our fate is sealed. There is nothing more to fear. Charlotte must chime in once more of course, "Now, you know."

"Yes, now I do indeed know."

"And I was right!" she mocks.

I knew she would like for me to try and back these very words, but all I gave her in return was a laugh for I could not have her believing in her looseness of thought. And so, we find ourselves in a familiar place, resembling our activity just a day or so before, only we have since switched our hands for a brush, and we no longer rip but we paint, a classic white to match the rest of the home. I am particularly fond of the walls, which seem so bare to Charlotte, as in every spare thought, she must insist on painting a mural onto the wall or ceiling, and each time I must remind her that neither she nor I have any sort of artistic ability, nonetheless an ability so profound I should want our work embedded onto my walls.

"What about just a willow tree, maybe a lake?" she asks contemptibly.

"Charlotte!"

She laughs, knowing she is only moments away from meeting my breaking point. "My dear, just paint. Remember whose idea this was exactly. And who graciously allowed you to do this much as it is." I inform her.

So, she does, painting away. One wall amassed in white. This time she moves to the left wall as I move to the right for us at some point to meet again at the very last wall. It must have been hours that have gone by as we have reached nearly the centers of our second walls; that is, until a knock is heard, echoing through the halls.

"That's odd, no one ever comes out here." Charlotte questions, pondering the idea of who it may be, frankly as do I, my mind with no choice but to flee to the notion of the peculiarity of our situation and who may be at the door may be a crack in each of our foundations.

"Don't worry, I will get it. You continue to paint."

She does, as I make my way around the corner and to the door where I attempt to evaluate the person's shape through the foggy glass. Small in size, but difficult to tell. The moment can no longer be off put, I must open the door. Turning the handle to what awaits, a moment of shock as I open the door to a young girl of Charlotte's age. I immediately set myself outside and shut the door for Charlotte not to hear.

"Are you one of Charlotte's friends?" I question.

"Um, not really. I was the one by the lake yesterday." she tells me.

"Ah, yes. I'm sorry, Charlotte yelled as she did. With all of the difficulty that has surrounded her, she suffers from paranoia. I'm sure you can imagine." I inform as jubilantly as possible meaning to mask the terror this young girl enlists in the fact the object of her being here, I have no inclination as to why.

"Yeah, well, you see, I need you to do me a favor." she nearly commands.

"And why is it that I should do you a favor?" I question.

"Because I could come up with quite the good story about things you and Charlotte may do."

"I am sorry, but you cannot come to my home and attempt to have me blackmailed, with your only threat being that you shall make up some stories."

"It wouldn't be hard. The town sees how you look at Charlotte."

This line, this is what I have feared. "What is this favor? Is it one that will make both of our lives easier because, quite honestly, I do not need to deal with a teenage girl running around spreading falsities!"

"I'm going to bring my parents over here and pretend that I'm staying here for the night. All you will do is tell them that I am staying here. When really, we both know there is no way I'd stay here."

"I do not believe I can do that. If something were to happen to you or someone were to find you while you were meant to be in my stead, I could lose my job. You have nothing to share that should scare me. But, if you should wish to spread your lies, I should too. I could imagine how you were one of Charlotte's biggest bullies. How you made her life worse than her father did, how even after losing it all, she is faced with your torment. You have no grounds, you see. You can attempt, but you should be prepared."

Her face is puzzled; I would hate to know how many families she has done this to because it would seem the last thing she would have expected to hear was a no in response.

"Fine. I just thought I would ask. I'll leave you alone."

Poor girl. She doesn't know what to do with herself. Could she truly imagine a grown man, the town's lawyer obeying her command when she has no real story to tell? Suddenly she stops on my last step to return for a moment to tell me, "I won't tell any stories because I don't need to. You don't go to town very often; you have no idea what people think about you two. I would be very careful about what you do."

And with that, she finds herself off again, and fear strikes once more. I would like to imagine simple people have simple imaginations, but in a town such as this, encased by people who have nothing better to do, the Lord may only know what type of stories they should wish to create to sprout drama from their town's dry soil. I realize now the town may think me her savior or her doom. Charlotte, no matter the case, should always be the victim in their eyes, as she lives in what seems to be an endless cycle of despair that stops at no end to fill her life. But what no one may understand is that when all they see is the Hell in my eyes, they cannot understand that I am only the Hades to her Persephone; a sorrowful man filled to the near brim with the pain from his childhood which seems to have never left him in his adulthood, a large fool who only wishes to possess the love of a girl he cannot have, a girl with such beauty and grace, silently she is filled with her own sorrow not visible to anyone as she dances in her fields of flowers in the sun. I watch from the shadows. She, Persephone—the only one to ever notice the beauty I have within myself. We both go unnoticed, in separate ways by anyone else in the world, that is, until we found each other. Although the world may say that I take her from her flowers and her sun and take her to the depths and pits where no one should ever dare to go, this is not what I do. I, instead give her all of the flowers which were once on the earth, the flowers with so much beauty and color at once in their lives but now rotted and unwanted; she, the only one to want the rotted, dark daisies, to make them beautiful. I give her a meaning to live. Why dance with the beautiful things when you can make something beautiful and dance with your own creation? Our lives have become intertwined to create the most complex of a situation as I fear of what one may think of me, of what I do to Charlotte, I can't help but to remember I had left Charlotte inside to paint as here, I still remain, outdoors, analyzing the holes which complete our empirical ballad. I must find her now. Not a difficult quest as she only moved a foot down the same wall, still paintbrush in hand.

"What was that about?" she can't help but to ask.

"I am sure you already took a peek out the window, so I will not lie to you. It was that girl from the woods at the lake. She had made an attempt to blackmail me if you could believe that!"

"Blackmail? Gosh. She has more thought in her than it looks."

"My mentality, exactly."

"So, what happened?"

"Well, she asked for me to tell her parents she was spending the night here while she goes off to do who knows what. I told her she only has stories, and stories do not constitute blackmail, and I will not be telling her parents anything of the sort."

"Huh, that's more than what I could have done. I probably would have stepped on the girl's toes and told her to leave. Spit on her even."

"Well then, I am glad I was the one to handle the situation."

"You and me both."

It is funny to me that time and time again, it seems Charlotte and I are both met with abhorrent situations, which again barely give us moments to breathe each time as they pass. We have overcome obstacles so tremendous one may laugh just at the thought of belittling the events to mere obstacles. As you can see now, here we are painting a room without any further commentary on the matter of the young girl who wished to blackmail me. I believe it must be the innate joy that deflects any deterrence before it can sink too deep into the matter of our hearts, which are only occupied by one another. With that being done, I should hate to bore with the further mundanity of painting, and I fear the day should bring little more adventure.

38

The sound of birds chirping, each chirp echoing softly in the room encompassing the window seal, the echo carried softly in the wind— nature's eternal alarm.

The days have gone back to how they were. I awake early, prepare myself for the day as silently as one may and await my dear, watching her rise parallel to the sun. As she wakes, she does not take long to get herself ready. She quickly meets me. Today I ask for her to join me on a walk, to which she agrees. She and I walk alongside the breeze, through the trees over the grass that holds the dew from the night. The children are all already at play, it seems they begin their journey into some far-off fairy tales much earlier now. I can imagine they are holding on to each moment of the summer before school begins again. It seems to begin so soon, just a matter of weeks. I haven't yet considered what will happen or how we should handle such a thing. That is a thought which shall only find itself in my nightmares for now. As Charlotte says, we have the summer at our feet, and so we still do. I should not cloud my mind with the pains of reality which have not yet breached our paradise. This is why we walk on a separate path from most; we walk alone, her and I only accompanied by what lies naturally beyond our home. Nature is silent, filled only with the sounds of the wind or a bird or two. Nature should never form harsh judgments or any line of dialogue; therefore, it should never tell one's secrets. That is why we leave all that we have to share at the foot of our willow tree for its roots to soak in and for our stories to remain locked within the world's natural safe. It is an inexplicable serenity to watch her hair, which resembles that of a rosy sun, fly through the air as Charlotte dances through the field; her feet, bare on the grass, her skirt fighting with the laws of gravity, and for her and her soundless melody to take in between her breaths a look into my eyes which she meets with a smile. She acts as the confirmation of our divinity. She, my angel, I, the most blessed man, captive in her holy grace. I ask myself each day how our love should be so forbidden if it was not for God himself who would provide us with each other's souls. We have reached the willow where we lay, her head on my chest for what could seem to be hours on end. We tell each other stories of our lives. We discuss politics and philosophy, history and mythology as she gathers my thoughts to protect her rebuttal with pieces of knowledge of her own. It isn't until hunger sits in, or the rain, or occasionally the downfall of the sun that we venture indoors; it is never for the lack of conversation.

Today we are met with sounds of thunder, and we decide it may be time to continue our work once more on the room. Having painted, we must begin the decorating process, as Charlotte calls it. However, it seems to be more of a repositioning party as it is a returning of its originally decorated inhabitants to the room only in different locations than before. Charlotte leaves before me across the yard, which takes you from our willow to our back porch. She glides through the tall blades of grass as I quicken my step, nearly jumping behind her, for I must not allow her to wait for me too long. We join each other, finding our way inside to shuffle portraits and furniture from one room to the next, reaching their decorative destination in the grand room. She decides by drawing out the visual design of where each painting shall be hung and precisely where each piece of furniture shall be moved. Attentive to detail she is, just as I. Although unexpected, as she can be quick to dive into her own creativity, she loses track of each of the small details which I must sweep up from behind her; it is obvious her passion overtakes her meticulousness. Whatever the case may be for her, she decides to map today before jumping in too deep, and so she does feverishly, drawing and erasing to redraw and crumble. I sit myself in the kitchen to take in my little love and leave her in her peace to her own imagination. That is until what sounds of a knock interrupts our peace. Another one to our very front door, which before this week had not offered so much mystery since Charlotte's return, and since has there never been a hand so pristine to brace that very door. Charlotte nearly immediately peered into the kitchen to look at me as though to inquire what emotion she should possess, whether it be fear or inquisition. Neither I could be the one to tell her as blackmail faced the door just yesterday; here, we face each other with blankness in our gaze to wonder who or what it may be now. I tell Charlotte to remain in the grand room as the shadow appears to be that of a man. I attempt to rationalize what man may await, but I have no inclination, nothing to tell myself, not the slightest of warning. I move slowly, so slowly it appears as upon finding the glass of the door, I see not a shadow any longer, though I still open the door to investigate the scene to which I find a letter left on the ground of the porch, and a man walking hastily down our drive.

"Excuse me! Sir, what is this about?" I call out in inquiry for the postman only ever leaves letters in the mailbox and would never once think to walk down my drive. I know I must have yelled out loudly enough as I can see the man fight with himself not to turn his head back to me. He makes no noise though, only providing me the ability to open the letter, which holds no notice on the front, not a single address from the sender or receiver. Regardless, I open the note to read:

"Mr. Hathaway,

The court would like to request the presence of Charlotte Thompson within the next two days between the hours of 9:00 am to 3:00 pm for important information regarding parental guardianship."

Being a lawyer myself, I cannot but frighten myself into wondering what news could possibly be shared with

Charlotte. At first thought, I would hope to take her right at 9:00 am tomorrow morning to learn of the secretive news, but I must rethink the possibility of her leaving or being taken away from my home. Should I pretend as though the letter was never received, burn it in its entirety or wait until the second day of the request and cherish each moment we have with one another until then. What could possibly be of the matter? Succeeding the duration of my own self-destruction, Charlotte came to find me, taking the letter from my hand to read it for herself.

"What's all the worry. I'll just go in tomorrow at nine and get it over with. Probably just some inheritance thing or something like that." she tells me.

She is right. It may be exactly something along those lines, come to think of it. "Yes, I'm sure it is something like that, but it is my place to worry for you." She leaves no reply, only she takes the letter, leading me back inside. "I shall take you tomorrow at nine then. Is that alright?" I ask her.

"Sounds good to me."

For Charlotte it came to me as no surprise to see she had not a change in pace as a result of the secret's becoming; I, on the other hand, cannot nearly breathe as I can only imagine the possibilities which may await us tomorrow morning. The greatest threat of all may be some long-lost family member who has come to take Charlotte away from me, or surely the court has grown suspicious of my love for her and believe her better suited somewhere else, away from me. At least, they can't put me in jail; I know that much. The only piece of my protection which hides me now is that they know I am a lawyer and not to fabricate their own laws for their own sake, but I know the rights each party holds. Only now, how they may use them is what remains the mystery. Quite frankly, I have come to a position where I do not know what is most bothersome currently; the idea of tomorrow or the fact that it is concrete, and Charlotte can sense my emotions from a light year away. It makes it all the more difficult to behave or act calmly when she already knows what thoughts have spent their lives spiraling through my mind. It is the difficulty in having someone who knows you so completely that not a thought may be shared, yet everything within you, you find laid before you.

She cuts in, "William, you have got to stop worrying so much. What's the worst they could say tomorrow?"

I do not know whether she wishes to further agonize my emotions or whether she has truly gone thoughtless to the idea of losing me. I imagine we shall go with the first option. The day has merely broken, and so the sun begins to crumble into an array of light cascading to darkness. Charlotte asks for me to read to her; she must have known what this would do to help calm my mind, relieving me of all pain, as it is driven out by the complex fullness of ecstasy. We lay, her body beside mine, fitting onto the small sofa in my office, her eyes watching the birds passing by the window as my voice echoes in her mind, leaving behind a sensation no softer than the touch of her hand, as she grazes my chest threatening the buttons of my shirt with each closer movement. By now, she has grown used to the quickening of my breath at her mere glance. It is but an evening which my mind has found an escape in my little love's grace, leaving all the worry for the morning, and the night for the walls of my home alone to fall witness to.

39

What the peace of a glorious night may bring in the forsaken morning. As I am awoken to the skin of my greatest love, I use my time to examine her beauty; laying beside her, I draw the lines of her face, internally to carry her very portrait with me anywhere I should go. I watch her as she begins to wake; I pretend to sleep as a test of her love. How should she choose to wake me? For now she only lays silently until, within the warmth of the morning, I am greeted by her cool hand upon my face. Slowly, I open my eyes as I look onto her entrancing beauty. She looks into my soul, the one which she is completely aware she holds, not in her hands but in her heart, she may find me entirely inside. Yes, you see, I am of her possession. It is a morning of slow awakening, with only so much time for our doom to catch up to us in our complete ecstasy. I have no doubt that, in some way, the worst of what life may have to offer us will find us at some time in our lives, whether it may be nine o'clock this morning, we shall see.

You see, the pain of reality is that you are only allowed to be happy for so long before any sense of joy must be diminished at its very root. Reality destructs the greatest of loves; it kills, it rots, it degrades, it leaves only ruins, yet we love. For what is life without love? This, I have learned in finding Charlotte. A life, my life, had only been lived in materiality; it had not been complete until I found love in Charlotte. As here, even today when we face the possibility of our ruin, our love shall not disintegrate; no, it only rocks, so that even if shattered to the ground, its remnants shall remain as statues of our affections. Our story shall remain through its audience. The willows shall be held captive by our story as our love provides more supply to its roots than water from the river. My thoughts should not hold time from moving on; 9:00 am and we are to be at the court. I may ramble, but we shall not be late in my reminiscence. Charlotte is here to remind me of the time, for she does not wish to be late either. Despite her vigorous attempts to cause me to believe she remains unworried, her sense of time management this morning should have me believe otherwise. So, just as it is nearly nine, we make our way down the path which we know so well, although much darker this morning. It seems to have grown grey in the night just to reflect the mood which we carry. We walk together down this path, for being one of such familiarity seems much longer this morning. Just one night and the world has seemed to change so. We continue our way to the forsaken place, a pile of bricks which should make claim to our very livelihood in just a matter of time, time which appears to be fleeing faster than my heart may beat with just moments until nine.

"Charlotte?" a woman calls out onto the porch where we have remained in wait.

"Yes."

"The chief officer is ready for you."

She takes that as her guidance to enter, and I follow.

"I'm sorry, Mr. Hathaway, but you cannot enter the room with her. You may wait here."

I, unable to enter the room, which should possibly decide her future? My Charlotte, she simply obeys! I, too, must continue my front as I am stabbed by the law upon Charlotte's tormenting eyes, which find me once more before her entering of the room. Her final breath taken while postulating in my wake, when I only wish to draw her into my chest; she is the furthest away from me. From beyond the walls which hold her captive, I can only hear the mumbling of voices.

It feels as if a century could have passed in her absence, that is, she emerges, immediately fleeing the men from within the room, finding my arms, and for the first time in a while, tears emerge from her eyes as she can barely gather her breath to inform me, "The— The— The jail is letting him go; they are letting him out! Please, please, you can't let him take me! You can't!"

"No, no Charlotte, you are safe. Please, tell me, what does she mean?" I look to the officers in succeeding my best attempt at comforting her.

"We are only liable to tell her." they inform me.

"Don't you see what this information has done to her? She is begging me to save her, yet she is so inhibited by emotion that she cannot tell me of what or by whom she needs saving!"

"Sir, we cannot."

"No! You must tell me, what have you said to her?"

No one inhabitant of this town has heard my voice raised to such an octave as until now, never had they seen my eyebrows crawl up as high upon my face, or my height grow as so. Therefore, only shock fills the room, out of it, though a voice, a female voice nearly silently sounds, "You, William, you could always take the case and then you would know everything."

"Excuse me?"

"You will be an official lawyer here soon enough, so all I must do is change the date on your contract, and you could pick up the case."

I look to Charlotte for a sense of security, though she only looks to me in bewilderment. Still, in knowing more than I, she holds only a look of exacerbation. The chief cut in upon having enough of our silent deliberations, I suppose, exclaiming, "What are you doing? You're going to change your contract to take on a case you know nothing about?"

"I will take on this case that I know nothing about in order to learn something, something that is obviously causing Charlotte pain!"

"Here, it's not very official, but nothing much here is anyhow." the office clerk chimes in once more.

"Except your policy concerning blood relatives being the only liable recipients of extraordinarily tremendous news. Where must I sign?"

She points eagerly. She reset the date of my contract to 7:00 am this morning, and with just the stroke of a pen, I have become official, a task I had put off in the name of love, now enabled much sooner in honor of that very name.

"As the lawyer on this case, will you please fill me in?"

"Then, Mr. Hathaway, here you are, Charlotte's father has reached his detention date, and so he has reached trial. Because he has reached trial, they can no longer hold him in jail."

"This is absurd! He has killed his own family and he should walk free. This will not hold up in court!"

"Mr. Hathaway, I was not done." The most preverbal words. "You see, he is going to trial and claiming insanity. This would mean the most he could be locked up in is a—
"

"I know what it means, hospitalized, that is all! The brink of insanity, which nearly constitutes the brink of freedom! Prisoners held captive in bars, but the worst of them, walking as they please through halls, past windows, onto their old homes, upon their old town."

"We know this must be upsetting to you."

"Upsetting? You all know what this man has done. Look at Charlotte! Look at what he continues to do to her! His 'madness' has outstretched his own arm's length; it finds itself creeping long past the jail's bars already, watching over his surviving lives. He will never be far enough away, yet he asks for near freedom?"

Charlotte has only remained in my arms through the entirety of the circus. Circulating tears, only igniting my anger further with her tears of terror that fall directly into my veins, igniting anguish. "Charlotte, look to me now. Hear my words, that man will not be let out of a cell for any second more of his life, not for trial, not for insanity. He will remain till only his fleshless bones can surpass him. You are safe. You will be safe." I attempt to comfort her. She is still unable to find the words to speak; she only hugs me greater than before, insinuating a thanks. The court knows my objective. They have now seen our love for one another. Whether they think it wholesome or damned; it is not for the care for there is nothing more than bars to lock with only my words as the key.

40

The worry which had ceased to cast its shadow upon Charlotte's face for so long had made its grand reprieve. The fear I see in her eyes blurs what angers me the most, that a man so heinous should attempt to walk free or that Charlotte is hurt. It is obviously a combination of the two, but I cannot help but wonder, without Charlotte, what I would feel of this man? Would this be just another case to fight? The night had allowed me to ask myself a skew of questions such as these; it was a night much like the ones lived when Charlotte first came to live with me. She made her attempt at bracing the darkness alone, but as the light faded and became saturated by the taste of despair, she found her way to comfort, which she found with me. Even still, the safest spaces may not stop the circulation of tears, all of which pained me more. This night further provided me with the motivation to face this man in court today. It seems astonishingly soon that we should be asking the court to dismiss the right for his return home while awaiting trial. It is quite astonishing they could find the pace at all, to be quite honest, but so they did, and as soon as he reached his detainment number, he set a date with the courts, who of course, have nothing else to do.

While I go into town today, I am not leaving Charlotte alone, though I am unable to bring her to face her father in the court, so I am giving her quite the list of errands to run and people to see to occupy her for the duration of the hearing. I know now that in the South, if you should find yourself unable to count on anything, you may always know that you cannot leave the presence of any southerner without a minimum forty-five-minute conversation. She should not be through for days if she were to reach the end of the list which I have created. 10:00 am is when the hearing is set, though I am to arrive early, sooner than her father could ever wish for. So, we are off. Just as she had lost the face of worry and had gained the ability to look upon her old home, today, she had regained not one manifestation of sorrow but two. I walk as I once had, holding her as tight as I may to my right side to block the vision of her agony, which should have been burnt down the night of the incident. It is in a time like this you wish to talk in a minuscule attempt to bring a sense of comfort, but in the moments that require the most careful attention, you lose sense of your words entirely. Perhaps it is that such careful attention is required that there is never a string of words so perfect that you should find the strength to speak them. Thankfully, this morning, nature proved its own distraction, for Charlotte found a pair of squirrels playing in the trees above to fixate her eyes. Although nature does not prove a distraction for the town who can find no other subject of their attention aside from both Charlotte and I; their eyes fixate upon us as we take that very step across that invisible line. I drop her off, imagining there is no more I can do as I know I will only be able to speak words of essence to her once again if I were to deliver her, her safety, and this is exactly what I set off to do.

"Good morning, Mr. Hathaway. You are free to get situated in the courtroom, the defendant will not be in until precisely 10:00 am, and he will remain under constraints until a verdict is reached."

"Thank you."

The courtroom is not much of what one may expect, just another room. One only that holds the decisions responsible for the lives of many: today, the life of my Charlotte, which has all of a sudden been taken up into my hands, God-granted by the courts. Every level of divinity had found itself now rooted in the ordained law. The clock mocks me as I cannot escape its grip, 9:58, 9:59, 10:00. He arrives. The time had come. Meeting his eyes at once, there is an immediate moment, a recognition that ignites a spirit in him I had not wished to bear witness to. He looks to his constraints as if to test whether they should truly hold him back in an attempt to advance on my life. We sit across the room from one another. I pay no notice to him, nor do I attempt to greet his eyes. The door opens once more, and there upon us all, the judge arrives. We stand and adhere to the typical legal proceedings for the 'judge' to begin,

"I call Wade Thompson to the stand."

He shuffles slowly to the podium, his lawyer (court-appointed and from a neighboring town I presume) with him. Funny thing, usually only the lawyer speaks for their client; not often do they take the trek together. It doesn't mean much to me, as it only has them appear even more foolish in the eyes of the judge.

"I ask that my client shall gain access to return to his home while awaiting trial."

With nothing more to say, he rests his head and returns them to their seats.

"Well, then, Mr. Hathaway."

The moment which lives rest upon, "Thank you, your honor. I wish to bring your attention first to the very fact that Mr. Thompson, who has just asked to return to his home while awaiting trial, has only just met his detention number, a detention which he was legally bound to serve as a result of a murder which he single-handedly carried out. The murder of his own wife, in his own home, in the night with no sign or witness to attest to a provoked rage. Mr. Thompson, here before us, is a murderer without cause. A second-degree felon under U.S. law. Not only in many states do such felons remain in jail until they reach trial, and throughout their trial, they quite often remain in jail for a greater number of years than they had even previously lived in their life. While I would hope your honor would entrust full respect to the law and the citizens within this town with all due respect to their safety, I would like to further mention the single witness to this horrendous crime remains in this town. Not only this, but the witness happens to be the daughter of the felon who has just recently killed her own mother just feet away from herself. She remains completely traumatized by the event and is without any family due to this murder. I ask you today that you take in account the heart of the young girl who has seemingly lost everything, and grant your protection over her by ensuring the continued detainment of the offender. Thank you, your honor." With the final nod of the head, I turn swiftly to address the horrid man with only a stupendous glare as he meets me with just the same, only, not with the eyes of victory as mine, but with anger, a maddeningly, increasingly angry gaze.

"The verdict is sealed. Mr. Thompson shall remain detained until a further verdict is reached through the entirety of trial procedure. If there should not be a verdict or trial, he shall remain in detainment."

I wave goodbye internally. Judges do not usually add so many details; it wages obvious he agrees with or without the evidence to compel him. Her father's anger had grown to such an extent I could feel his hands reaching for my neck as he was nearly fully departed. I could barely cease to look him in the eye; how could anyone, especially Charlotte, bear to do the same. Oh, Charlotte, I must tell her the news immediately. Escaping the court as quickly as possible through the commotion of the office, pleading to allow myself to leave to tell Charlotte the news. I find her just making it to her third destination on the list, heading into the pharmacy, as I had expected of her. Just as she begins to open the door, I call out to her; immediately upon catching my eye, she allows the door to fall back on itself to run to me for the news. I'm not one to fake solemness to excite only moments later as a means building excitement for the news, so I tell her immediately, "Charlotte, it's done. He will be locked in that cell until a verdict is reached, and if one Is not reached, he will still be locked in that cell!"

With a breath of relief, she jumps to me into a hug; I can nearly twirl her around due to the level of joy she bears upon me in finding me again. In putting her to the ground, she questions, "So, what will the verdict do? I mean, can it set him free or give him only a little bit of time?"

"You know I do not tell you lies. The truth to trial is that a verdict may mean anything can happen. Nearly anything can be tried, by law, but that does not mean everything will not fail. It is quite obvious the judge, as impartial as expected, is not a fan of your father, nor is the rest of the town who will serve as jurors. Charlotte, you are loved and cared for beyond an eternity surpassed, though I am not sure their hatred may meet closely. It may all be chance, but I can promise you; your safety has the better chance. Today should act as proof."

"That seems right, but you will still be taking this to trial, right? You will still be the lawyer?"

"Is that what you would like?"

"Yes, yes. It is what I would love for you to do."

"Then I shall do it."

And with only a hug to suffice for a thank you, though suffice is a dragging understatement for the reimbursement, I should be responsible for paying for all the life she gives me in just one touch, in one hug.

We go home today more grateful for each other than ever before. Although unimaginable, it had been done, and with that, one another's touch has never been more cherished. This day though joyous in the end, still is enthralled by a breeze of worry; as the sun falls below the ground, it seems not just the longest day has come to an end but that we shall be reminded of the days to come. Today, a triumph; tomorrow, only up to endless possibility. Regardless of chance, it is a stress which walks between us down our drive and follows us into our home; the idea of the possibility which lingers inconspicuously. What a shame it is that to further cherish the love you hold, it must be wavered by horrible possibilities. Yet, no matter the state of our lives currently in the balance held above it, we join each other in bed, I read to Charlotte into the night with her in my arms, and as the shadows grow larger, creeping towards us in our comfort, we share the protection of each other's hearts, which should, when intertwined, create the greatest force fathomable.

With just twenty minutes more, "Goodnight, William."

"Goodnight, Charlotte."

I place my kiss upon her forehead for her to let herself go into my arms, and off to sleep she goes.

41

My patient audience, if you are still there, I bid a good morning to you. Today, I have come to find that you never realize how lovely of a world it is until you love the only person who makes the world, to you, a little less lonely. This is what it is for me to leave Charlotte, for me to lose her for just a day, just an hour; it does not matter for if she is without me, and I, without her; I am lost. Left to the world's consumption, my heart taken from within me by the hunger of the world, leaving me to my lonesome self. Incomplete. The morning I bid to you as good, only reminds me of the hours I should spend without Charlotte in my wake in the office, figuring up a case. I wake to her beside me, to her keeping me as full as a man can be but awake to the eyes which hold me hostage to my own bidding. I took this case for Charlotte, but it is at her cost that I must fight for her joy. What a paradox the world has made out of us, one which shows me into a pit comprised of my own despair from nine to five. The morning once complete, now lost for good as I wander into my civil office. Still, the congratulations flow from my cohorts, but what has been done launches no comparison to what lies ahead. I lock myself in my case to work out each very detail, to find holes in legal text, to comprise my words which I should hope shall damn him to Hell. But all that is done in a lonely day may just be worth the greetings I meet upon entering my door from my dear, nonetheless. She knows not to ask at my work, or of the case or of anything of such a matter; she knows it is painful for us both, so instead, we spend the time in each other's wake doing the activities we love the most with one another. It may not be of any surprise, we read, we walk, we watch the stars on the porch as the sun falls and as the night rolls in, and as the wind becomes cool enough, we open the windows and lay in my bed to talk for what seems to be hours on end— a routine which loses no satisfaction but keeps me breathing until the morning comes again, and I face the pains of reality sun after sun.

42

In dreams, I float into an ethereal of my own creation, one in which willow's branches blow, reflected in a shallow meadow beneath the sun. In mornings, I awake, today with the sun risen upon Charlotte and I's blissful bodies at peace within one another's arms; the sun shines to declare it is time for me to prepare my departure. So, I begin to topple out of the bed; Charlotte, who I had thought to be asleep, grabs my hand, most mornings she does not wake so soon, but her eyes reach up to mine and she asks for me to stay with her just a few moments more. I pull myself back beneath the covers and she rests her hand on my chest for her to feel my each and every breath. She moves in closer to me. We lay with our hearts beating upon one another's to the same melody. She knows now it is past time for me to leave, but she does not allow my exit; rather she places her lips upon my cheek and in their departure, she whispers, "I'm sorry."

"Sorry for what, my dear?" I ask her.

"For all that you have to go through with this trial. It is because of me."

"You are right. It is because of you. Charlotte, it is all because of you, because I just so happen to love you."

I do not know what could have possessed me, whether the morning air had intoxicated me, but for some reason, the words which I have not dared to say, the three words which have fought for departure from the day I met Charlotte, just simply made their escape. As I remain to my own vulnerability, awaiting what she may say in return— her eyes, they ponder, her lips almost quiver, "You love me?"

"Should I not?"

"No, William, I—I love you."

She loves me! Charlotte, my greatest of love, my glorious Persephone, my fate, my doom. She loves me! 'I love you.' That is, she loves me. I want more than my heart's content to breach her lips, to fulfill our love, but our love is one of peculiarity, uniquity, which society does not make room for. Charlotte and I are exceptions to the normality of love, but society does not make room for exceptions. And so, I wrap her in my arms for her to know her love is safe with me.

"I wish you didn't have to go."

"I wish I could stay, but as much as it pains me to leave your side, I must go. This case requires much work. I will be back soon enough, my dear."

It has come enough time, and so she allows me to go. I file out the door, across the porch which encases the founding of our love; I fade into the willows, lost to the town, to find a means to maintain her safety. And in the silence which surrounds me, on a morning as serene as the feeling of solitude, I find in the eyes of my Charlotte, I question the peculiarity of our love, the love we love, both her and I, in equal return. And so, I believe it is the insaneness of it all. Maybe the hopelessness. Is it the enchantment, the utter beauty, the joy, or is it the brutality? What love must confine a man to the grip of a young girl's heart, which he may never possess? What cage I have built for myself. What euphoria has blinded me only to surround me in walls of inclination with no doors for passage? My life—saved and destroyed in one summer.

Reaching the office offers no passage to the answers to these questions; I am only left to my work. I wonder how I could not but win this case. Every spare thought of mine is consumed by the possibility of a loss, but just how should this town allow this man his break even if he were to claim insanity? How must I even think to properly establish the details of my case after such a morning, after she, which has filled me with ecstasy! That is it! That shall be my case, my opening address,

"Ladies and gentlemen of the jury, what you shall find before you is a case of a man who in his own narcissistic rage shot his wife, the woman he had vowed to love, the woman whose hand he took, yes, the woman whose head he held a gun! And in not a moment of insanity but of perfect calculation, he pulled the trigger, which rid him of a fellow being, a human being who drew attention away from himself. To win the love of who in return? His daughter? He killed her mother in front of her very eyes, just meters away, and he left his daughter with not just a brother who has passed on but a mother, tragically murdered in her childhood home surrounded by only the terror of the wretched night. Not even insanity can possess a man to do such a heinous act! If you should believe it insaneness due to the irrationality or to the spontaneity, this man is not one who casts his brutality onto his family in just a night; no, the only path of consistency which he vowed to follow in his life was that of consistently leaving his children home alone to care for their mother, only for him to return home drunk enough for them to care for him as well. Their money—taken from their very hands to support a life of his own. The life of this man and of his children has remained bilateral from their very birth, yet when in the moment their lives did cross, they suffered the anxiety of pondering whether they were on the brink of a fist or of the pain that his voice instilled. Insanity does not behave so consciously to the public yet turns itself on right as it walks through its home's very door! No, insanity is not an excuse for drunkenness or absentness or cruelty; it is a method of quick release. And to what? Wreak havoc among his daughter's life once more, should he be released so quickly to take care of his last piece of baggage he has left behind? This man does not need his mentality protected, but this man has a daughter whose life should need protection." I am quite good, am I not? Perhaps I am not finished, "Ladies and gentlemen of the jury, I wish that you should not look so far to see the selfishness within my act of accusation, putting my dear Charlotte's father behind the bars that should contain him into his eternity. I shall so solemnly swear that I do not wish only to keep Charlotte in my arms but to seek justice for a cruel vileness that previously walked inconspicuously among us all. I understand you should ask what the world is without a father, but jury, you are unaware, Charlotte has already filled this hole—"

My weightless banter receives interruption— outside the office, I cannot but hear the commotion, the yelling in the streets. Quite odd for so early in the morning. Quite odd for any time of day here at all. Other than for this instance which I am working to dissolve at this moment, there is never but a raise of voice in this town. Is that thudding I hear? The sounds of someone forced onto a wall? I can't help but allow my curiosity to take control, leading me to abandon my work; I fold my clean papers over the ones which occupy my most satire address. Turning the hall, I immediately become pushed back indoors by my fellow colleagues.

"What is of the matter?" I question, attempting to contain my alarm.

"You cannot go out there!" they warn.

"Why must I not?"

"It is not safe for you; trust us, please!"

"This is absurd!" I exclaim.

"William, please, stay indoors!"

I try again, forcing my way out the doors, but I am unable to even reach the corner to the doorway as everyone in the office has come to push me backward, "Please, you have to stay!" they inform me yet again.

"Why?"

"It is unsafe for you."

In the distance, I hear the name Charlotte ring just as a man may have yelled for her. Why else must they keep me indoors away from some apparent danger when Charlotte may be in the midst of it. A strength came upon me in the instant her name could dissolve in its echo; no number of office staff could further prevent me from taking my passage outdoors to the center of whatever crisis may be in wait. I rush out into the crowd, "Charlotte!" Just as I could allow such an angelic name to outrun my tongue, a methodic noise interrupts me, a stream of screams, as my ears ring not with the voice of my darling but of a bullet dislodged from a gun. Maybe I am no longer in Georgia at all, for the sound of such a gun places me back in Nottingham as a young boy, foxhunting alongside my father. The sound of gunfire cannot have threatened my very solitude as I awake from my transport to the face of a man, one of unique familiarity, but it couldn't possibly be... Charlotte's father. The screams of men and women alike attempt to battle the ringing of the bullets in decibels. Have I faced the day? His face seems to disappear behind the light of the sun, which shines ever so bright. With that, the sun so high in the clouds, I fall to the ground just as the sun does before the moon may take its place. As my face meets, just as the rest of my body, the cool ground, the dew still remaining from the night, I may find a moment of peace; the gun with not a bullet more, and the screams ceased. This is not until the sounds may begin again, only not like before. No, I can hear a wailing, a lonesome cry, far in the distance! Yes, it must have been a house so silent she could hear her own heartbreak; with that, a bullet must have found the other half of my soul! There it is. I've come to the point where I feel no more pain; our two souls have conjoined again, hers lost just as I have lost mine. She joins me as we fade far away into our new world. And so, is it down from the Heavens or up from the Hell flames that I see, I do not know, for with Charlotte paradise surrounds me, but there, a replaying of my world before me, yes; it was love in the morning and in the evening. It was love on the grass and on the gravel. It was love in the river and in the lake, on the steps of our porch, in our home, and on Main. It was love when we walked with her hand in mine and when she ran through her fields of flowers even as her hand nearly escaped. It was love beneath the willow; it was love that was carried within the wind. It was love. The greatest of love. That is the story of Charlotte and William. William and Charlotte. Though even the greatest of stories must come to an end, and as I watch our love replay, I can see Charlotte and I both buried beneath our willow tree, the one in which its branches once blew, giving off the air in which she breathed. And in the wind beneath the willow, Charlotte and I may finally be at peace.

EPILOUGE

Read only if you do not believe in happy endings

It is not, but even one murder you wish for in a town such as this. Two in a summer; our new resident, the victim of a bizarre tragedy. Today, the day an inmate escaped, tracking down his opposing attorney, and now here lies William Hathaway in the middle of Main, his body remains. The women in tears, the children at loss of their words; they only tremble as their fathers keep them at a distance. Only one may never stay far enough away.

An awful sight interrupted by the passing through of a one young girl who is in an attempt to meet a friend of hers for an answer to the commotion, a strawberry blonde not but the age of seventeen.

A friend calls out to her, "Charlotte, here! Here I am! It was your father; he escaped."

"You mean he did this?"

"Yes, he, your father.... Well, he killed a man."

"Killed who?"

"William, your neighbor, you know the attorney."
"Oh, yes. I met him once."

That shall be the end of the story of William
Hathaway.

www.ingramcontent.com/pod-product-compliance
Lightning Source LLC
Chambersburg PA
CBHW022037240626
47154CB00007B/2448